DECRYPTING THE CACHE

THE GEOCACHING MYSTERIES, VOL. 1

by Jennifer Kirsch

Cambridge Books
an imprint of
WriteWords, Inc.
CAMBRIDGE, MD 21613

First Print Edition, August, 2016

Publisher's Note: This is a work of fiction. All characters and events, treasures lost and found, portrayed in this book are fictional, and any resemblance to real people or incidents is purely coincidental. Geocaching, however, is a real pastime enjoyed by thousands of people, on six continents. Therefore, all geocaching techniques used and all web sites mentioned in the story are based on actual sites.

Cambridge Books is a subsidiary of:

Write Words, Inc.
2934 Old Route 50
Cambridge, MD 21613

ISBN 978-1-61386-353-4

Fax: 410-221-7510

Bowker Standard Address Number: 254-0304

Dedication

For Thomas, Linda, and Anya

CHAPTER 1

Treading through a shadowy woods didn't rank high on my fun list. Yet I found myself surrounded by tangled tree limbs and hairy vines one Sunday evening. My new friend Dev crept along with me as we navigated angry roots, sprawling branches, and knotty trunks that resembled our knobb-nosed history teacher.

We hoped to find a geocache. "You know," I'd explained to Dev, "a hidden container you find using a navigation app." But he'd wanted to see it for himself.

Dev made a face as we passed a smelly, rotting stump. I glanced over my shoulder, trying not to dwell on reports of bears in these woods. *Beep*. My phone signaled that we'd approached the cache.

"In there?" Dev pointed to a massive, cracked boulder on the trail's edge.

"Probably. Let's grab it, then get out of here."

Cobwebs and shriveled leaves filled the crack. Dev hoisted himself up. "Maybe the view's better from the top."

I dug around in my backpack for a flashlight. When a twig snapped, I shuddered in spite of the steamy weather. Usually geocaching was fun, not creepy. Would Dev ever go again?

"Erin?" Dev's voice came out an octave higher than usual. His darkish skin had paled.

I followed his wide-eyed look to the ground. Then my head jerked back. A skunk now stood guard at the base of the boulder.

"Don't panic," I whispered. "We'll figure something out." But I had no plan.

"Maybe I can climb down over here." Dev still sounded like a soprano on helium. He peered over the side, only to spring back. "Poison ivy." He checked the other side. "Here, too. And it looks like someone watered and fertilized it all summer long."

I gulped. He'd never hang out with me again. And he was the only nice person I'd met since the school's new scheduling system had separated me from my friends.

"Any ideas, Erin?" Dev gnawed on his fingernails, moving from one to the next, like eating corn on the cob.

Maybe I could lure the skunk away with a pretzel from my backpack. The beast only hissed at my offering, though. Then it arched its back. I quit breathing. The taunts of kids at school filled my head. Long after I'd scrubbed, aired, and deodorized myself stink-free, their jeers would echo through the hallways. Two weeks into eighth grade, I'd be branded the Stench Wench for the rest of my school career.

Retreating a step, I started edging around the boulder. "Maybe there's a way down in the back." Still on tiptoe, I reached the other side. Robust, prize-winning poison ivy covered it.

I twisted one of my monster curls. Either I'd soon smell worse than a Dumpster, or I'd break out in a maddening rash. And gathering clouds gave me little time to decide between the two.

A glance toward the front told me Dev had finished off the last of his fingernails. His fingertips might soon disappear. And the sky kept growing darker. Instead of fluffy sheep, the clouds now resembled ravenous monsters gearing up for an attack.

Sucking in a huge breath, I took action. It probably meant showering ten times that evening and burning my clothes, but I chose skunk.

* * *

The churning clouds rumbled as I crept back around the boulder toward the skunk. Just when I reached the front, ear-splitting thunder rattled the air. The animal spun its head and snarled, its tail now raised on red alert. I shielded my eyes and crouched behind a mildewy stump.

Adding to the fun, fat raindrops pelted my shoulders. But then another thunderclap exploded, and the skunk bolted into the thicket.

A long breath escaped my lips. But I didn't break into a victory dance, because my troubles hadn't disappeared. In fact, compared with everything that had gone wrong in the last year, skunk spray looked like a picnic.

Dev scaled down the boulder, doing Twister moves to sidestep the vines strangling the sides. "Whew." He brushed himself off. "I couldn't see anything from the top. You're sure the container's in there?"

"Absolutely." A glance at my phone confirmed it. "The coordinates I got off the web site are pointing right to the boulder." I tried to sound upbeat, despite the rain. Part of me still worried Dev would relocate to Antarctica if the skunk made another appearance.

"I think I see something metal." Dev leaned way over to peer into the crack. "And it's filled with loot?" He licked his lips.

"Exactly." The description on the web site had listed a bunch of stuff. "The online logs said it has some night vision goggles." I didn't mention that they were probably plastered with pictures of Resh Renner, every little kid's favorite action hero.

Dev reached in. His tongue peeked out of the corner of his mouth as he poked around. Finally he pulled out the cache—a sturdy, shoebox-sized container. "Cool!" He brushed off the dirt and cobwebs.

We huddled under a rock outcropping and opened the lid. Inside, we found a few foreign coins, a plush banana slug, some windup chattering teeth that jumped at Dev's touch, and a wooden box. I dug deeper, catching sight of a Resh Renner decal on something plastic. But it turned out to be a peashooter, not eyewear.

My stomach knotted as Dev riffled further. He found a spiral notebook, but no goggles, even though the cache description had advertised several pairs earlier that weekend.

I flipped through the notebook, scanning the most recent logs, and then chewed on my lip. "Someone beat us here."

Several visitors had recorded entries within the past few days.

"They must have taken the goggles." Avoiding Dev's gaze, I uncapped the attached pen and added my mark to the soggy page.

Dev pulled the peashooter out of the cache. Gunfire chirps burst from his lips as he targeted a tree trunk. "I'm taking this," he said, with a shrug.

I raised my eyebrows, surprised he'd want something with a Resh label. But then he blew some paper pellets in my face, making me laugh. I also exhaled. Dev no longer looked ready to set sail for Antarctica.

But other worries remained. In fact, I felt like a whirlwind had ripped through my life in the past year. First Dad lost his job. Then he took a temp assignment in Hawaii, half a world away.

Dev bombarded me with more pellets. I swatted them away as I picked through the cache again. The wooden box caught my eye. Actually, my eyes probably bugged. The box's bottom had a sliding panel.

"What's that?" Dev glanced up from reloading the shooter.

"Not sure." I slid the panel open.

"Cool." Dev leaned closer.

Behind the panel we found a hidden compartment secured with a miniature padlock.

My skin prickled. "Locks protect valuables."

Dev slurped up some slobber. "You think there's something inside there?"

"Don't know." More thunder rumbled as I gave the box a shake. I opened its lid but came up empty. Flipping it over again, I stared at the lock on the false bottom. What did it hide? A diamond, maybe. Or a rare stamp that would buy me a plane ticket to visit Dad?

Rainwater dripped off the end of my nose. The wind picked up, sending rotting stump fragrance our way. "Come on. Let's go." I put the box in my backpack.

"Can we keep this, too?" Dev held up the peashooter.

"Sure." I dug through my backpack. "Standard geocaching policy is, 'Take something, leave something.'" I pulled out some goodie bag favors left over from my brother's last birthday party and stuffed them in the container.

Dev fired off a final round and stowed the shooter as I returned the cache to its hiding place. With rain hammering down around us, we hurried back to our bikes and pedaled home, every spin of our tires splattering suburban mud up our backs. I barely noticed, with thoughts of gems, rings, and rare coins swirling around my head.

* * *

Back in my family's apartment, Dev and I pored over the box. Its lock showed letters instead of numbers, and it had six dials.

Dev flipped the box upright and studied the bird painted on the lid. "*Feather*?" He twisted the first few dials but then stopped. "No. Too many letters." He gave it another turn. "*Twitter*?" He frowned. "Still too many."

I scratched my head. The bird didn't look anything like the robins and blue jays we had in New Jersey. Instead, it had bright red eyes and black and white wings. "How about *winged*? Or *birdie*?"

Dev tried both. Neither freed the loot.

I opened the box's lid. My head snapped back when a few fuzzy notes rang through the air. "I didn't hear any music in the woods. Did you?"

"Probably the thunder drowned it out." Dev closed and opened the box again. It simply replayed the same short tune, six notes in all.

"It must have an embedded sound chip." I peered inside. "What's this?" A flat piece of metal was wedged into the bottom. I pulled it free but realized it resembled a dog tag. My insides twisted.

"Something wrong?" Dev inspected the lid.

I fidgeted. "We can't keep the box." I handed him the tag. "See this id number?" I pointed to some engraving in the metal. "It means the box belongs to another geocacher."

"What?" Dev examined the tag. "I thought if we left something in the cache, we could keep it."

"Usually you can, but not if it has a tag." I stared at the metal plate and slumped. "It's supposed to travel from one cache to another. The owner tracks its movements online."

"Bummer. But I can keep this?" He hugged the peashooter to his chest.

"Exactly." I started to question his infatuation with a Resh Renner toy but stopped. It had kept him from getting bummed about the goggles, after all. "But we need to move the box to a new location and update its position on the web site."

Dev's eyebrows shot up. "Nothing's stopping us from opening it first. I don't know about you, but if there's a microchip in there with passwords of foreign bank accounts, I'm finding it."

My head tilted to the side. "True." I reached over to the computer, no hard task in our cramped living room, and went to Geocaching.com. The following information popped up, once I entered the number on the box's tag.

Magpie Box
Owner: The Bird Watchers
Released: Thursday, 10 September 2009
Origin: New Jersey, United States
Recently Spotted: Spooky Hollow
Current Goal: Travel east.
About This Item: A wooden music box.

"Magpie Box?" Dev studied the lid. "Is that a magpie?"

"No idea." I checked the date on my watch: September 14. "Someone must have just put it in Spooky Hollow—the cache in the woods—a few days ago."

"Hey, *magpie* has six letters!" Dev grabbed the box and spun the dials. I held my breath as he aligned the last one, but nothing budged.

Back on the box's page, I clicked on a link marked *Add a Log Entry* and started typing.

Picked up this box in the woods.

Before hitting *Submit*, I added another line.

Will carry east within a week or two.

"At least we'll go geocaching again soon." Dev had read my log entry.

"That's right." My family wouldn't go, like we used to. In fact, I'd have more luck finding a cache inside an active volcano than going on a family trip anytime soon. Mom now worked full time, and Dad couldn't join us for outings, or even dinner, at the moment. But at least the skunk hadn't spooked Dev into never going again.

Still poking around Geocaching.com, Dev clicked on The Bird Watchers, the user who had launched the box.

The Bird Watchers
Profile Information: I wake with the lark song, hopefully before the swan sings.

"Huh?" I read the description again. I'd heard of larks and swans, but neither had six letters.

"What's this?" Dev pointed to a link labeled *Send Message*.

"You can e-mail other cachers through the site. We could ask The Bird Watchers about the combo." Bird watching didn't appeal to me, though. I could easily name two hundred better ways to spend an afternoon. Still, we needed to open the box.

Scrunching up my nose, I clicked on the link and typed a message.

> *Hi, The Bird Watchers. I picked up Magpie Box in Oak Creek Woods but can't figure out how to open it. What letters should I enter?*

"Let's hope they get right back to us," Dev said. "And not tell us they've lost the combo or hidden it in the woods in the nest of some rare bird."

* * *

At school on Monday, I thought about the lock all day. I even had a few good ideas until Mrs. Dearg crumpled up my history paper scrawled with six-letter combinations.

In band, when Mr. Weber went into a long lecture on concert pitch, my head buzzed with more bird-related words.

"Erin Schmidt?" Mr. Weber cracked his gum. "Are you with us today, Erin? Or is your mind still on summer break?"

I cleared my throat and sat up straight.

"Erin." Mr. Weber stooped toward me as he switched to a kindergarten teacher voice. "If you play a C-sharp on your saxophone, what pitch is that on a piano?"

I knew the answer—three half steps up from C-sharp, or E. But before I could say it, Mr. Weber waved his baton and called on someone else. The whole experience made me forget all the letter combos I'd come up with.

At lunch I scanned the cafeteria, hoping to spot a friend, or at least someone I knew from rec softball. But just like the first week of school, no one looked familiar. Only Pierce stood out. The hulk-bodied brute, who captained the school chess team, was targeting random kids with globs of Jell-O.

When his launcher swiveled in my direction, I sat down at Dev's table. I didn't care if Dev chewed with his mouth open or burped after each bite like some boys. I just didn't want Pierce spotting me alone and making me his next victim.

"Did you open that padlock yet?" Dev asked, as if he could see letter combos swirling around my head.

"Nope." I poked at my multi-grain mac & soy cheese. "No luck yet."

"I wonder what's inside." Dev shoveled pomegranate-chia yogurt into his mouth. "It might just be a packet of birdseed, you know."

I stared in disbelief. Did Dev actually like the school's New Age food? "No idea. But why lock it, if it's not valuable?"

Dev tilted his head from side to side as he drained his yogurt. "As a joke, maybe?"

"If there's even the slightest chance it's worth something, I need it. I'm saving up for a ticket to Hawaii."

"Hawaii?"

"Yeah, my dad lives there."

"Oh." Dev looked up from unwrapping a flax seed scone. "Are your parents divorced?"

"No. My dad lost his job last fall—"

"When the economy fell apart?"

"Exactly. He just started an assignment on Hawaii last month, excavating caves. He's an archaeologist."

Dev choked on his scone. "Any chance you're moving there? To Hawaii?"

"No, it's just a temp position. We're staying right here, in Northlawn, New Jersey." I thought of our tiny apartment, the place we'd called home since last summer, when we'd lost our house.

"So you just want to visit him?"

"Right." But the last time I'd checked flights to Hawaii, my savings had barely covered the fuel taxes and baggage fees.

"So what are we waiting for?" Dev licked flax seeds from his fingers. "Let's crack that code."

"I had a few ideas this morning. I'll try them after school."

"No, I mean literally. Forget the combos. Let's use an ax." Dev stood up and mimed swinging a hatchet as the bell rang.

CHAPTER 2

The wooden box beckoned when I let myself into the apartment later. I couldn't concentrate, though. My stomach growled, reminding me I hadn't finished much of my birdseed macaroni. Next, the sounds of a game show's buzzer and the cheers of a studio audience drifted through the walls from the next apartment. With all the noise, I couldn't remember anything I'd thought of earlier.

Then Mom and Marcus came home. I'd just flopped down on my bed, only to hear Mom yell, "Erin! Saxophone!"

Uh-oh. I'd used the leaky key excuse for days and had barely practiced all week.

"You have a lesson at school tomorrow, don't you?" she yelled, over pots and silverware clattering in the kitchen. "Now, please, before we eat!"

Blowing air from my cheeks, I got up and stuffed a reed in my mouth. When my songbook fell open to the most syncopated etude ever, I collapsed onto the edge of my bed. I felt like sliding all the way to the floor. But I didn't. Instead, I squared my shoulders and dug in, going over the rhythms again and again. I needed to finish practicing, so I could get back to the box. Its code was my only link to Dad.

Finally the syncopation came out right. "Yes!" I jumped

up and threw out my arms like a gold medalist. As I sank back onto my bed, the bell of my horn banged into the wooden box, knocking it over. Its lid opened, activating the sound chip.

Once it finished playing, I shut and opened it again, listening to its song.

A funny tune, very short, it almost sounded as if something were missing.

I picked up my sax and blew out a note, trying to match the box's first pitch. After experimenting a little, I pinned it down: an E. I listened again. The melody began slowly, lingering on a high note. Next it jumped around. At the end, it dropped lower, turning sad. After a few tries, I managed to find all six notes: E-A-B-D-C-sharp-F-sharp.

I snapped my fingers. The tune itself could be the key! Those six pitches might open the lock.

The first dial already read E. I twisted the second, third, and fourth letters to A, B, and D. Then I stopped. C-sharp came next, but the lock only listed letters, not sharps or flats. I shrugged and turned the fifth dial to C and the last one to F. I took a deep breath and pulled on the lock.

It held fast.

I stamped my foot and stared blankly ahead. I probably looked as confused as a caterpillar that had crawled out of Marcus's pocket after a hike one day, completely disoriented, as if it had feasted on the wrong kind of mushroom. After a minute, though, I tilted my head to the side. What had Mr. Weber said in band? Something about concert pitch? Mostly I remembered him putting me on the spot. Still, maybe the transposing idea had some merit.

I grabbed a pencil and scribbled down the note sequence on the back of my algebra sheet: E-A-B-D-C-sharp-F-sharp. I had to count on my fingers, but I managed to transpose everything to concert pitch: G-C-D-F-E-A. Spinning the dials once again, I entered this new melody.

I gasped. The latch had clicked and slid open.

For a few seconds I sat, paralyzed. Finally, I peeked inside the tiny compartment.

I slumped. It appeared empty.

I took a closer look, though, and found a thin roll of paper, tightly wound and crammed against the box's edge.

Carefully I pulled it out. Weathered and crumpled, it looked like it had gone through the laundry or maybe even a forest fire. Bits of its charred, frayed edges rubbed off in my hands.

Faint handwriting looked up at me from underneath a layer of glitter after I unrolled it. I brushed it off, creating a shower of sparkling gold powder. Underneath, I deciphered the following scrawls.

48'
18'
Opal

"Forty-eight, eighteen, Opal?" I read out loud. "What?" I stared at the note, hoping something would hit me.

Nothing clicked. The numbers and the word made no sense, and the tick marks didn't help. A single quote usually stood for feet. Did the measurements give the dimensions of a building?

I scanned the note again. Then my eyes rested on the word *Opal*. Dad had once given Mom opal earrings. Maybe someone had hidden a jewel in an abandoned building. My mind bursting, I pictured chests of gemstones, glittering pendants, and jewel-studded video game remotes. If the code led to riches, I'd see Dad again soon.

Marcus's footsteps sounded from the hallway. The cardboard-thin walls in our apartment at least gave us advanced warning of everything.

He poked his head into my room. "Wanna play *Resh-opoly?*"

"Sure." I actually would have rather worked extra algebra problems. But today, who cared if I wasted an entire hour losing to Marcus's space stations and intergalactic ports? My head was reeling with the wooden box's message.

* * *

"Coordinates are measured in degrees north or south of the Equator and east or west of the Prime Meridian." Mrs. Dearg's voice droned across the history room the next day.

I tried to look interested, taking notes on the tablet computer on my desk. Still, I couldn't concentrate. *Forty-eight, eighteen, Opal* plagued my head.

"Degrees can be further split into minutes and seconds." Mrs. Dearg's appearance didn't make it any easier to focus. In fact, she resembled a cartoon caricature with exaggerated features: a large, knobbly nose and bright red clown hair. The neon green leg warmers she wore also did little to tone down the comic look.

Dev brought me back to the present. As Mrs. Dearg turned her back to the class, he sent an instant message to my tablet.

Hey, Erin. Did you get the box open?

I flipped back a page in my textbook, pretending to check a fact. Then I turned to the screen and tapped in a reply.

> *Yup. I found a note inside that said 48' 18'*
> *Opal.*

I hit *Send* as Mrs. Dearg continued her lecture. "To convert from the first form to the second, subtract the decimal part of the minutes, which ends in a single quote. Multiply it by sixty to get the seconds, whose unit is abbreviated with a double quote."

Within seconds, Dev replied.

> *Opal? Sounds valuable. Can you show me later? Maybe we can hit some balls at the park, too.*

I flashed him a thumbs-up as Mrs. Dearg raced to post as many facts, names, and dates as possible to the board before the bell rang.

After school, Dev and I got in some practice throws at the ballpark. Afterward, we headed to my apartment to work on the wooden box. But Dev wouldn't stop drooling over Marcus's extensive stockpile of Resh Renner spy gear. I shook my head. I might not be the most girly of girls, but I would never understand boys and their action hero infatuations.

Finally, back on the geocaching web site, we opened the box's page. Dev poked around. Then he clicked on the link leading to The Bird Watchers' profile. It still listed the same vague statement about waking with the lark song. Next he opened the *Trackables* tab.

"Trackables?" he asked. "What are they?"

"That's just another word for things that hitchhike from cache to cache, like the wooden box."

"Well, The Bird Watchers own two other trackables. Maybe one of them can help us decrypt the message."

I looked up. "I wonder if there were any more trackables hidden with this one."

"In the cache we found the other day?"

"Yeah." I took the mouse. "I don't remember seeing any other ID tags, though." I opened up the cache's page on the web site. It didn't list any other trackables, but Dev explored the embedded map and discovered two other geocaches in the woods, one on the southern end and one on the western edge.

"Let's go south first." He clicked on the southern cache. A description popped up, along with some statistics. "It has a few trackables. One's named Macaw Box. What was the name of this box? Something about a pie?"

"Magpie Box." I did a double take. "Macaw Box? That sounds similar. Who launched it?"

Dev followed Macaw Box's link and landed on its home page. "The Bird Watchers released it just a week ago!"

I scanned the screen. "And its goal is to fly south. I wonder—"

Dev held up his hands to cut me off. "Hold on a sec, Erin. Let me get this straight." He cleared his throat. "The Bird Watchers launched the box you have—Magpie Box—in the cache we found on the eastern edge of the woods."

I nodded.

"Since it's a trackable, you can't keep it. Instead, you need to move it east."

"Exactly." I nodded again.

"At the same time, they launched another trackable—Macaw Box—in the southern cache, sending it south."

"You're catching on fast."

Dev smiled and maybe even blushed. "So, how much

do you want to bet the cache on the western end has a trackable that's headed west? It's probably named after some bird native to the West, too."

Dev brought up the description of the western cache. He slumped in his chair when the inventory read, "There are no trackables in this cache."

I twisted one of my monster curls, which resembled loose springs, ready to recoil with a *boing* if someone tugged on them. "I wonder where the other one is."

"Doesn't The Bird Watchers' page list which trackables they own?"

"No, I don't think so." A brief tour of the owner's profile confirmed my suspicions. The page only displayed the number of trackables The Bird Watchers owned, not their names. "Wait a second." I returned to the western cache. "Let's check the inventory history."

Dev clicked on the cache's *See the History* link. The screen listed the trackable items that had visited the cache. Right at the top appeared Quail Box.

I grabbed the mouse and clicked on the box's link. Then I jumped up, toppling my chair. "Look! The Bird Watchers own it!"

"But its current location is someplace called Suburban Obstacle Course."

"So it *was* in the woods, but someone named Fife & Drum moved it to another cache."

Dev wagged his head and held up his hands again. "You're losing me."

I set my chair upright and then opened an online mapping site to draw a sketch.

"There are three trackables, all launched by The Bird Watchers." I pointed to the map. "Magpie Box in the East, Macaw Box in the South, and Quail Box in the West."

Oak Creek Woods

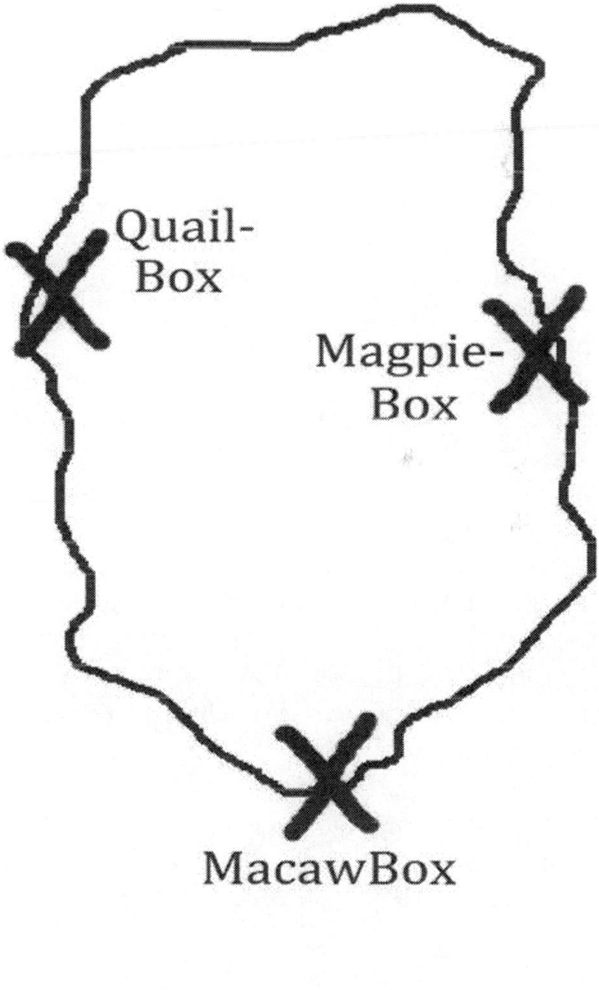

Dev nodded.

"I've got Magpie." I held up the box. "And it's heading east. Macaw is still in the woods, but it's supposed to go south. Then there's Quail. It was in the western cache but is now in another cache called Suburban Obstacle Course." I clicked on the link for Suburban Obstacle Course. "Which is in Hilland, a little to the west."

I zoomed out and updated the map.

Dev studied the drawing. "So if we could track down Quail Box or Macaw Box, they might give us more info on Magpie's secret message. What did it say again? Something about an opal?"

"Forty-eight feet, eighteen feet, Opal," I read off the already tattered scrap of paper I'd copied the message onto.

"Then what are we waiting for?" Dev grabbed the mouse and expanded the map.

"Nothing. But hold on a second."

Dev looked up.

"If these boxes lead to valuables, I need my share for a plane ticket. But what's in it for you?"

Dev's eyebrows shot up. "Who'd say no to treasure? But also—" He hesitated. Then his cheeks turned red again. "I don't know. What's not to love about a mystery? Plus, anything's better than hanging out with my boring family." He turned back to the screen. "Let's start with Quail Box in Suburban Obstacle Course."

Tugging on a curl, I stared at Dev. When he didn't elaborate on his plans, I turned to the map. "Actually, I've been wanting to go there."

I pointed at Suburban Obstacle Course. "That's a new cache, a multi, and it's not too far from here."

"A multi, as in multiple choice?" Dev scrunched up

his nose. "Please don't remind me of Mrs. Dearg's tests. I never know which answer to pick. The choices are always equally likely."

I smiled. "No worries. The cache is easy. We just choose all of the above."

Dev didn't look convinced.

"It's just a series of caches hidden in different locations," I explained. "Each has a hint for finding the next. The stash is hidden in the final stage."

"Cool. I'm all for it." Dev looked at his watch. The excitement then faded from his face as quickly as Mrs. Dearg could write "latitude and longitude" on the board after hearing the final bell.

"It's late. I've got to go—some anniversary dinner for my grandparents. But let's hit the cache tomorrow."

"Sure." I held out my hand for a fist bump.

* * *

Our plans fell apart before we even got started. Dev needed to get a cavity filled after school the next day, and my mom had scheduled errands for the afternoon.

"I left work early so we can take your sax to the shop in Oak Creek," she announced once I got home. "It needs a tune up. They close at five, so let's get going."

Hanging my head, I let my backpack fall to the floor with a thump. About to kick the closet door in frustration, I stopped. The woods with Macaw Box was in Oak Creek! Before Mom could herd me into the car, I found the cache online and entered its coordinates into my navigation app.

First we dropped off my horn.

"There's a cache in the woods right across the street," I yelled to my mom over honks and squeaks from a beginner sax class. "Can we get it?" I held up the phone. "I already programmed it."

She squeezed her temples and nodded. She might have agreed to bungee jumping in that moment, just to escape the painfully out-of-tune "Hot Cross Buns."

I opened the app and practically skipped toward the trees. Marcus was humming along with the saxes. The tune would probably stick in my head for the rest of the week, but I didn't care.

Just a few steps into the woods, I heard someone call my name. I turned to see a boy with dark, wavy hair standing on the sidewalk next to a woman dressed in a sari.

"Dev?" I called out.

"Hey, Erin." Dev crossed over to join me on the trail. "Do you think the macaw box is still in that cache?"

"Yeah. We were just going to look for it. Do you want to come with us?"

"Can I, Mom?" Dev asked the woman. "We're all done at the dentist." He gave his jaw a tender pat.

His mom shook her head. "I need to get back to the shop." Her elegant accent didn't disguise the firmness in her voice.

"You must be Dev's mother," my mom said. "I'm Julie Schmidt. We can drive him home later."

When Dev's mom agreed, he and I led my mom and Marcus through a swarm of gnats and down the path.

For several minutes we meandered among dangling branches. Then the app beeped. "We're within a hundred feet." Hearing a buzzing sound, I looked up and came to a stop as a wasp circled us.

"They only sting when they're upset," I whispered to Dev. "If we don't move, it won't bother us." The two of us stood stock-still, waiting for the creature to whiz out of sight.

"A hundred feet?" Marcus yelled, clearly less educated

in wasp etiquette. "Let me see!" He grabbed my phone as the wasp performed several loop-the-loops around him. Then he forged ahead with his eyes locked on the screen, nearly stumbling over some gnarly roots.

My mom's phone rang as Dev and I set off behind him.

"Erin, keep an eye on your brother. I'll catch up in a few minutes." She stepped to the side to take the call.

We soon reached the southern end of the woods. The app beeped again. My heart fluttered in response.

"We're really close now." I surveyed the scene and smiled confidently.

Marcus spoiled the moment. "The first time Erin went geocaching, she couldn't find the container," he taunted.

"That thing only measures with an accuracy of twenty feet." I pointed at the app. "So we had to search a pretty large area. We looked up in trees, under bushes, through leaf piles—everywhere, but couldn't find anything."

"She had to write, 'Didn't find it,' on the online log."

I scowled at Marcus. "After that we started checking the hints given on cache web pages."

"Hints?" Dev asked. "What did the hint for this cache say?"

"Timber!" My smile returned. Directly in front of us lay a felled tree.

While Marcus poked at something to the side, Dev reached into the log. He frowned. Then he grasped my hand. "Your wrist is tiny. See if you can reach anything."

My fingers trembled as I stretched my arm in, thinking of the macaw box, nearly within my grasp. I kept probing for metal or plastic as my mom caught up with us, still strategizing about project plans and high-level meetings into her phone.

"Sick! Cool!" Marcus jabbed a stick at a hollow tree.

Dev copied the idea. He found a branch and poked it into the log. He and I pricked up our ears, hoping to hear a tap or thud that might indicate a container. Meanwhile, my mom went on about budgets and schedules on her phone. Unfortunately, nobody paid any attention to Marcus's comments about rows and rows of perfect hexa-things. His questions about the name for shapes with six sides also didn't set off any alarms. We simply reached further into the log, brushing against something solid and rectangular.

"Aaagh!" All heads jerked up, however, when Marcus let out a bloodcurdling scream. Several angry wasps zoomed out of the hole in the tree he'd poked and descended upon him.

"Run for the car!" my mom yelled. She grabbed Marcus's wrist and pulled him toward the path while a voice called out of her phone, "Everything all right, Julie? Hello?"

Dev and I scrambled to our feet as several wasps jetted toward the log.

"Still think we should remain calm?" Dev asked. "I'm not sure, but I think that one might be giving us the finger." He pointed at an approaching wasp.

"Forget what I said!" I bellowed. "Let's get out of here!" All thoughts of the wooden box forgotten, Dev and I joined Mom and Marcus in hurdling roots and pelting down the trail.

None of us escaped sting-free, and the entire way home, Mom glanced nervously out the car windows. It also occurred to me that Marcus's screaming might prompt someone to call the police. But I didn't dwell on it or the painful welts. Instead, I worried what Dev thought. With his ears covered, he sat, staring out the window. If Marcus didn't shut up soon, Dev might never hang out with me again. I couldn't afford to lose the only friend I'd made at the middle school.

When we'd nearly reached Northlawn, Dev turned to me. "Are we there yet?" he mouthed, while nodding at Marcus. He then smiled and winked.

I let out a sigh of relief. Dev might still like Resh Renner, and he might be a boy, but I was glad to have him as a friend.

Chapter 3

"Hello?" Mom answered the phone when it rang after dinner that evening. Then she stopped, mid-stride. "I thought there wasn't any cell coverage in the caves. Oh, are you in the office today?"

Before she could say another word, Marcus grabbed the phone. "Dad! You'll never guess how many wasp stings I got today! There's even one on my butt!"

I raced into the family room and picked up another phone.

"There are five total on my left arm!" Marcus continued. "The biggest one is an inch wide!"

"Ouch," Dad said.

"Dad," I said. "I went geocaching the other day, and—"

"And you should see the size of the ones on my neck!" Marcus interrupted.

"Ouch," Dad said again.

"Dad, I found something geocaching."

"I already started making my Halloween costume!" Marcus blurted out. "I'm going as a gargantuan bowl of macaroni and cheese. I'm collecting toilet paper rolls, and I'm painting them orange to be the macaroni. Do they have toilet paper in Hawaii?"

"Of course we do, Marcus." Dad sounded exhausted.

"When will you come home again, Dad? In time for Halloween?"

"Uh... I... I don't know, Marcus. I can't say for sure right now."

"Maybe you can help me paint everything and put it together!"

When Dad stammered out another vague response, I hung up the phone, escaped to my room, and let my door slam. I sank onto my bed, scheming about painting Marcus's macaroni a moldy green color. But my plans got sidetracked. Something sharp was poking into my leg, as if the wasp stings hadn't already tortured me enough.

I rolled over and found a dinosaur fossil. In this cramped space, it must have fallen off the heap of junk on my desk and onto my bed.

Its rough surface tickled my fingers. I'd gotten it on a geocaching trip in July, the last time my entire family had gone caching together. Instead of wasps, we'd run into ants that day. Several had zigzagged around the log hiding the cache. Instead of a cell phone, Mom had held a flashlight. She'd aimed it into the end of the log. Reaching in, she'd suddenly shouted, "Ow!" and jerked out her hand, shaking it.

"Fire ants!" she'd explained. Marcus and I had scattered, though I thought I'd caught Mom winking at Dad. Laughing, Dad had then pulled a metal box out of the log and flicked a harmless carpenter ant off its lid.

Inside, buried under about a hundred marbles, we'd found several plastic bags. Each was neatly labeled "One Hundred Fifty million year old dinosaur bone," and held a hard, pointy fragment.

My lips began to widen into a smile as I relived that fun summer day. It faded as the whine of some neighbor's electric guitar brought me back to the present and I thought of the wasps buzzing in the woods.

My shoulders sagged until I remembered Uncle El. He might know what to do.

I pulled out my phone and began typing.

Erin: You there?

I drew my knees up to my chest and wrapped my arms around them.

Uncle El: ?
Erin: I found a note in a trackable. It said 48 18 Opal.

A few moments of silence passed. I waited.

Suddenly, I inhaled sharply, as a flash of brilliance struck.

Erin: Maybe 18 is the opal's weight, like 18 karat gold. Do opals have karats?

I hit *Send*. But right away I sensed how unglued I sounded. A weight alone wouldn't give the stone's location. Plus, the forty-eight remained a mystery.

Thoughts of Dad pushed their way to the front of my head. I pictured him and me opening the macaw box, which I'd nearly had my hands on. We might have already decoded its message. Dad would have checked out the wasp nest, too. He would have kept Marcus from poking at it. He would have shown him how to watch it quietly, from a safe distance. Together, they would have oohed and aahed at the symmetry of its hexagonal cells.

Erin: Life is more fun with Dad.

Dad always let me and Marcus try out workshop ideas for Slivers and Shards, an archaeology camp he ran during the summer. We went on more family trips, too, and found better loot while geocaching, like the dinosaur bones. Mom also joked around more, pretending to be stung by fire ants, instead of going on about deadlines and budgets into her cell.

A lump formed in my throat as I thought back to the phone conversation. Dad couldn't even give us a firm date for his next visit home. I opened my calendar and counted days. He'd been gone for seven weeks. Soon my fastball would be slower than Marcus's, and I'd have trouble telling apart pottery pieces and arrowheads I found on hikes.

Like gas passed in an elevator, my gloom surrounded me, with no sign of fading.

> *Erin: If only some massive volcano would erupt on Hawaii. Then the caves might fill with lava, and Dad would come home.*

Finally, a response came.

> *Uncle El: How about a round of "Lost"*

I hadn't played "Lost in the Labyrinth" in a while. I'd spotted Dev on it the other day. But for me, Resh Renner video games had lost their appeal years ago, along with dolls, playground slides, and freeze tag. With a shrug, though, I found the game's icon and hit *Play*.

Resh appeared on my screen, trapped in a life-sized maze. I needed to search for pieces of a map showing the way out and then steer him toward the exit.

Midway down a long, narrow path, I heard the chirp of

laser fire. Aliens had appeared at both ends of the passageway, surrounding me. I dodged their fire and made Resh dig, hoping to unearth a safety pack hidden in the ground. Nothing appeared. The aliens closed in. I dug deeper.

Whirr, whirr, whirr!

"Yes!" I pumped the air with my fist.

Just in time, I'd found a hover-mobile token, good for a temporary lift out of the maze. Not only would I escape the attackers, I'd also glimpse a rare overview of the labyrinth.

But I couldn't focus on the winding paths as Resh rose up in the air. Instead, I gazed into the distance. Beyond the exit lay a lush, green valley. Traces of pink etched their way into the horizon as the sun prepared to rise and flood the land with light.

Thud! The hover-mobile depleted its power source and dropped Resh back into the labyrinth's recesses. His head whipping back and forth, he waited for direction.

I shuddered. No aliens lurked in the shadows. All the same, an eerie feeling had crept up on me.

After pausing the game, I switched screens.

> *Erin: I'm lost in a labyrinth, like Resh. I don't know which way to turn, like I'm stuck in a life size maze. Without Dad's help I don't know what to do with the wooden box.*

The way out of Resh's labyrinth clearly led to the safety of a peaceful valley. Still, I didn't see how any good could ever come from my parent's separation. Worse, I doubted their marriage would survive the time apart. I didn't know much about mortgages or credit ratings, but even Marcus had picked up on the tension in the air over the past year as financial worries had intensified. The fact that Dad couldn't nail down a date for his next visit made everything worse.

Erin: I don't see a way out.

I shook my head and sat with my arms tightly crossed over my chest. After a minute, I flipped back to the game. On-screen Resh waited for the next command.

My phone buzzed.

Uncle El: Just in: an upgrade. Can load while playing.

Seconds later, a link to the newest version of "Lost" arrived in my e-mail. I hit *Install* and urged Resh on. He meandered among the pathways, dodging new, more menacing monsters. Shiny objects appeared, as well. They glittered as they reflected light, resembling miniature magnifying glasses.

I made Resh pick one up. It led to a shortcut. Zigzagging along, I collected more. Soon, I'd worked my way to the exit.

The next screen threw me a curve ball, though. Instead of an ultramodern shuttle, a minivan stood just outside the labyrinth, waiting to transport Resh to central command.

I leaned forward. The car looked a lot like my family's van. Where had Uncle El picked up this upgrade? The rear fender even had a slight dent, identical to the one on our car. He must have doctored the imagery himself.

Looking past the bizarre special effects, I turned to the horizon. It now glowed bright pink. As the minivan sped toward it, I couldn't help thinking of the promise it seemed to hold. I opened another text window.

Erin: The magnifying glasses make me think of clues. Maybe if I follow the trackable clues, I can navigate my own maze.

Admittedly, I faced an impossible task. Still, I could at least try to reunite my family. I could almost picture my dad and mom, Marcus, and myself, together in the minivan on the bright horizon.

I opened the map I'd made showing the trackable boxes.

Erin: There's another box in a woods cache. Tomorrow I'm biking there & finding it.

Assuming the wasps didn't remember me and unleash their anger, I would start piecing together the clues immediately.

Uncle El seemed to agree.

Uncle El: Over & out.

* * *

Unrelenting rain kept me from visiting Oak Creek Woods the next two afternoons. When the sun finally came out on Saturday, Dev and I met at my apartment. We meant to set out right away, but the geocaching web site reported that Macaw Box had moved south.

"We practically had it in our hands the other day!" I said. "I can't believe it's gone!"

"Yup," Dev read off the screen. "Someone named Rather Be Fishing picked it up on Thursday."

"Thursday? It was pouring Olympic-sized pools of water that entire day!"

"I guess the bad weather made for good fishing. They

dropped it off yesterday afternoon in History Geek's Delight, wherever that is."

"It must be farther south than Oak Creek. Macaw Box is supposed to go south." I clicked on History Geek's Delight. "It's a mystery cache. We can't really tell where it is."

"A mystery cache?"

"Yeah. You have to solve a riddle or figure out some clues to get the coordinates of the site."

"How hard can it be?" Dev grabbed the mouse and scrolled down.

We came to the following information:

> *History Geek's Delight*
> *The cache is* not *located at the published coordinates. Instead, it can be found at:*
> *N 40° A' B"*
> *W C° 17' D"*
> *A = Arthur + Wilson + Taylor - Tyler*
> *B = Johnson + Tyler*
> *C = Pierce + Arthur + Harding + Polk*
> *D = Harding - Hayes.*
> *North Checksum = 88, West Checksum = 28.*

"How does this work?" Dev asked. "Do we replace the letters with numbers?"

"Right. I think the words somehow translate into numbers. Once we figure out which ones, we plug them in to get the coordinates."

"What's the checksum part all about?"

"It's just there to make sure we're not way off track before we set out. If we add up the digits in each line, the sum should match the checksum for that direction."

"Hmmm." Dev stared at the puzzle again. "The words look like names, and they all seem familiar, but I can't remember where I've heard them before." After another minute Dev shook his head. "Let's check on Quail Box." He took the mouse. "It was in a multi-cache somewhere the last time we looked."

"Good idea. In fact, we can put a watch on it. Whenever the box moves, we'll get an e-mail with the new location." We set up the watch with a few more clicks. We also learned that Quail Box still lay undisturbed in Suburban Obstacle Course.

"Obstacle course?" Dev asked. "Do we get to scale mountains and zip-line over rivers?"

"Probably swing over some quicksand pits and do some rock climbing, too. Let's get going."

* * *

We reached Hilland in no time. The navigation app led us to a playground in a park. After poking around, we found a mint tin attached by a magnet to a fence. A slip of paper inside listed some coordinates and read, "*A* = number of playground ladders."

"We need to count ladders here at the playground?" Dev asked. "Then go to the next address?"

"Exactly. With a multi-cache, you find a series of containers, and you usually have to collect information along the way. You use it to get the final coordinates."

We split up to count ladders, all the while avoiding a screaming toddler. Some kids flinging sand at each other had showered the little guy. His baby-sitter didn't seem to care. She just sat on a bench, drumming on her knee and bopping her head to some music while fiddling on a humongous phone.

The new coordinates and the clue "no pain, no gain"

then led us to a lamppost surrounded by trash bins and thorny bushes. We checked underneath a few foul-smelling cans while avoiding prickers on the hedges. Finally we found a small container under the light's base. Following its instructions, we fanned out in a nearby parking lot, hopping over concrete parking stops as we counted the "number of spaces" to find the value for *B*.

"Uh-oh," Dev said. The toddler from the sand pit had just run into the lot. Mimicking Dev and me, he also started hopping over speed bumps. His baby-sitter followed at a distance, still entranced by her phone and tapping a beat with her fingers. I'd never seen hair quite as long as hers. It reached past her waist.

"Let's get moving," I said when the kid fell, scraped his knee, and started bellowing again.

I led the way to the third site. The hint "bench coach" helped us locate the cache, a miniature plastic container shaped like a wad of chewed bubble gum. Magnets held it to the underside of a bench in a ball diamond's dugout. I extracted the log and then wiped my hands on my jeans. I'd tugged on several genuine globs of used gum before finding the cache.

"And this formula will give us the final coordinates, where the quail box is hidden?" Dev asked.

"Exactly." I studied the note I'd found in the cache. "But first we have to find *C*, the number of swings in the park."

"Swings?" Dev scanned the area. "There aren't any around here."

"I think I remember some back at the entrance."

We turned to go just as the toddler appeared on the scene, still whimpering.

Back at the entrance, we counted swings. My heart

thumped a little faster. At last we'd have the address of the final container. We'd get hold of Quail Box and unlock the mystery of forty-eight, eighteen, Opal.

I plugged in the information we'd gathered at each step. Finally, I entered the final coordinates into the checksum, only to find it didn't check out.

We probably looked as deflated as a leaky kickball that lay abandoned in the grass. The oppressive heat didn't help. Still, we retraced our steps to the parking lot to recount spaces. When we came up with the same total as the first time, we trudged back to the sand pit. This time around, we discovered some rungs hidden inside a play fort.

"If we count this ladder, we get six instead of five." I shook sand from my hair. The kids were now engaged in an all-out sand fight. "With *A* at six, the sum checks out."

Even though we'd hiked, climbed, and jumped all afternoon through the obstacle course, thoughts of Quail Box propelled us toward the final stage. Soon we found ourselves in a field behind the playground, where a small gazebo stood.

"The hint says, 'Switch headlights on,'" I said.

"Headlights?" Dev asked. "Oops. We forgot to bring our car."

"But the only place you could drive a car around here would be up that drive." I pointed to a gravel road that led to the back of the gazebo. "It must be hidden in the back somewhere. I've got a flashlight. Let's take a look."

Just inside some lattice panels, we located a small container. I held my breath as I opened it. Dev reached in first, pulling out a handful of stuff. Soon he and I had covered the ground with a few foosball men, a manatee wearing a flowery bathing cap, some frayed friendship bracelets, and a plastic bag filled with googly eyes. We dug deeper. Finally we pulled out the logbook. A panicky tremor then shot through my insides. Underneath it, only a few worn erasers shaped like pumpkins and a shiny medallion littered the bottom of the container.

"There's no box!" Dev moaned. He sounded like the networks had cancelled Resh Renner's TV show. "No quails either."

Chapter 4

I peered into the container and gave it a shake. Then I sorted through the junk on the ground. No quails materialized. Our hope of decoding Magpie's message dissolved, melting faster than a chocolate bar in the sun.

"Someone must have come earlier today and taken it," I said.

We checked the log book. Three other geocachers had recently visited the cache: Rather Be Fishing, Fife & Drum, and Chain Cacher.

"Rather Be Fishing?" I asked. "Fife & Drum?"

"Those names sound familiar."

"They do. I think they each took a box from the woods."

"That's right," Dev said. "They must be after all three boxes, too."

About to nod in agreement, I stopped short and hit my forehead with the heel of my hand. "That cranky toddler! His baby-sitter had some kind of sophisticated, ginormous phone, but maybe it was an old navigation receiver!"

"They kept following us around the park, but you think they were geocaching?"

"Yup." I examined the container again. "And it looks like they beat us to the cache. And took the wooden box while they were at it."

"They probably got the ladder count right the first time, with their inside knowledge of the play equipment. And they must have known the number of swings without having to retrace their steps."

"Or some other geocacher took it." I glanced at the logbook in my hand.

"Good point. At any rate, the race is on. We're not the only ones tracking the boxes."

Dev picked up the container. "Look at this." He lifted out the medallion we'd seen and held it up by a chain attached through a hole near its edge. About the size of a quarter, the disk shimmered in the warm sunlight. "Rather Be Fishing," Dev read aloud.

"It's probably a signature item," I said. "Lots of geocachers have tokens printed with their user name. They leave them in whatever caches they find."

"Cool." As it swayed in the breeze, its image of fish and waves changed color, moving from a deep blue to a metallic green shade.

"You can keep it, if you want. Some people collect them. I brought some vampire fangs Marcus got from our dentist. We can leave them in its place."

"I'd rather have the quail box, but at least it's something." Dev pocketed the coin after another look.

"We might as well sign the log while we're here, too." I opened the on-site log book and entered *Water Break*.

"Water Break?" Dev asked with a smile.

"Yeah." I felt my cheeks heating up. "I didn't choose that name. My mom did, years ago, when Marcus couldn't hike more than a few minutes without begging for a break and a drink of water."

After replacing the cache, we trudged back to our bikes. "We can check the online logs later to see where Quail Box is off to," I said. "And in the meantime, let's try to solve the mystery cache and reach Macaw Box."

"What do you mean?"

I pulled a slip of paper out of my pocket. "I copied down the names listed in the puzzle."

Dev took the sheet. "Arthur, Harding, Hayes, Johnson, Pierce, Polk, Taylor, Tyler, Wilson."

We stared at the list. "Oh!" I snapped my fingers. "They're names of presidents! We had to memorize them once in school."

"Oh, yeah." Dev studied the list. "But how can presidents translate to numbers?"

"Not sure. Maybe their time in office has something to do with it." I scratched my head. "Nah. That would involve too many numbers."

We reached the bike rack. "Maybe you just replace their name with whatever number president they were," Dev said. "Washington would turn into a one, Adams a two, and so on."

I cocked my head sideways. "I think that's it!"

While cycling back, we passed a cinema in Hilland. A huge ad featuring Resh Renner hung in its window.

"Hey, I've been wanting to see that movie." Dev peered up at the listings.

I looked around. Did he really need to broadcast that fact?

Dev let out a growl. "But it already started while we were hurdling parking stops and scaling play equipment."

Hoping no one from school had spotted us, I pedaled away and urged Dev to follow.

Back in my apartment, we logged our visit to the cache. We also checked Rather Be Fishing's latest log:

> *Found this pretty bird today. Will drop it off quite a ways west of here on next fishing trip, toward the end of the month.*

"So Rather Be Fishing took Quail Box?" Dev asked.

"Yup."

"I wonder if that's the baby-sitter. I bet she's onto the mystery, too."

I opened Rather Be Fishing's profile. A photo of a balding, heavyset man greeted us on the next screen.

"Either she started wearing a Rapunzel wig and lost a lot of weight since that picture was taken, or that's not our sitter," Dev said.

I squinted at the screen. "Hey. I know that guy! I was at a geocaching event last year with my family. We met some other local cachers, and he was there."

"And look. There's his signature card." Dev pointed at a sparkling graphic on the page. He fished the coin he'd found earlier out of his pocket and compared its image to the online display. "Same design. So the baby-sitter must be someone else. Probably Fife & Drum."

"Which makes sense." An image of the woman popped into my head. Her long, blond hair swayed from side to side as she twitched to a beat. "She kept tapping out some rhythm."

We checked Fife & Drum's profile but couldn't find a photo.

"Anyway, I wonder what Rather Be Fishing wants with Quail."

"Right. 'Quite a ways west of here' doesn't sound good." I chewed on my lip.

"Is there some way to send Rather Be Fishing a message through the web site?"

"Yeah. Sure." I frowned as I thought of the e-mail I'd sent The Bird Watchers, which they'd never answered. "But what about Macaw Box? Let's see if our idea of replacing the presidents' names with numbers works."

"Let's also hope Fife & Drum doesn't get to it first."

Dev consulted a textbook. "Tyler is president number ten, Polk is eleven, Taylor gets twelve, Pierce is fourteen, Johnson: seventeen, Hayes: nineteen, Arthur: twenty-one, Wilson: twenty-seven, and Harding: twenty-eight."

I entered everything into the formula spaces on History Geek's Delight's page.

"Woo hoo!" Dev gave me a high-five. "We got valid coordinates!"

Dev stopped his victory dance when we scrolled down the page and checked the cache's inventory. Macaw Box had moved on.

Fife & Drum had taken it earlier that morning. She'd posted this log:

> *Have another macaw trackable that's entered in a race of bird trackables going to the Caribbean for the winter. Will deposit both in a cache south of here in a few days.*

"So let me get this straight," Dev said. "You've still got Magpie, but it needs to move east. Rather Be Fishing's got Quail, and it's heading west. And Fife & Drum now has Macaw and is sending it south."

I nodded.

"So basically everything's slipping away."

"And we're not the only ones after them." I chewed on my lip and clicked through several menus. "Let's set up a watch on Macaw Box, so we can track it, too."

"Sure. Then if we happen to have a spare afternoon, we can jet off to the Caribbean to pick it up." Dev looked bummed for a second. Then he smiled. "At least I'll get out of my aunt's wedding."

* * *

That evening I e-mailed Rather Be Fishing. Before Macaw or Quail ventured any farther, I needed some answers.

> *Rather Be Fishing,*
> *I'm interested in Quail Box. Do you plan on dropping it close by anytime soon?*
> *Water Break*

I checked for new messages every minute on Sunday, if not every second.

Rather Be Fishing got back to me fairly quickly.

> *Water Break,*
> *So you're interested in Quail Box? Then I suggest you check the logs. I don't believe in passing trackables directly from one geocacher to another, but I'll tell you this: I'll be taking it fishing next Sunday and will drop it in a cache sometime on the trip.*
> *Rather Be Fishing*

I deleted his mail. Then I opened the map I'd made and added a big red arrow next to Quail, pointing west. I'd already drawn one heading south for Macaw.

* * *

My in-box held me under its spell the next few days. On Tuesday it finally delivered some news.

"Fife & Drum dropped off Macaw!" I shouted over the phone to Dev as soon as I saw the mail. "It's in a cache called Karaoke Candy."

"Karaoke Candy? Where's that?"

I zoomed out on the map. "Somewhere on the south side of Oak Creek."

"Is it anywhere near Kid Kingdom? My little sister went to a princess party there last week."

"No idea." I scrolled through the cache description and jotted down the coordinates.

"Hey, my mom said something about making a delivery in Oak Creek today."

"No way."

"Yeah. I'll ask if she can drop us off. Call you back in a minute."

Dev's mom agreed, and within half an hour, we'd entered Kid Kingdom, navigated a maze of mini arcade games overrun with kids on sugar highs, and sighted the cache. We had to wait to get near it, though.

"Geocachers try not to attract attention," I explained as I dodged a ball misfired from a ball pit fight. "Otherwise, people might trash the caches or mess them up."

"This whole thing makes me feel like Resh Renner." Dev ducked to avoid getting sprayed with silly string. "We use modern technology to make a secret exchange at a previously agreed upon location while trying to blend in."

"True. We even use code names."

"Right, Water Break." Dev winked.

I felt my cheeks burning. Leave it to Mom to choose such a stupid name. "Hey, have you set up a geocaching account?"

"No. I... Um... I haven't decided on a name yet."

"What about Certifiable Hottie?" I raised my eyebrows. The previous week, a straight-haired girl had sauntered over to our lockers. Flashing Dev a smile, she'd announced that she and her friends had placed him among the top ten in their list of hottest boys. She'd then turned to me with slit eyes and given me a once-over before flipping her sleek strands and sashaying off.

Dev's lips curled into a smile. "You're just jealous because you wish you had nothing better to do than coming up with stupid lists."

I couldn't help smiling, too. After hearing he'd topped a list, Dev hadn't signed any autographs or made plans to hire an agent. Instead, he'd simply slipped off to the boys' room, clutching his stomach.

Another ball flew out of the ball pit. Then a scratchy voice boomed through the speakers: "Maintenance has now cleaned up the accident. The free fall is working again." The area cleared in no time as everyone ran for the ride.

Dev and I got down on our knees and crawled between a karaoke machine and a cotton candy stand to reach the container. Not caring why the carpet felt sticky, we sat down behind a garbage can to look through the cache.

Right on top we found a box with a bright tropical bird painted on it. Dev flipped it over. Underneath, a sliding panel opened to a letter padlock. I grabbed the box and opened its lid. A few notes rang through the air, although we had to crane our necks to hear them over gunfire from a shooting simulator.

"How are we going to figure out the pitches?" Dev asked.

I couldn't help grinning as I reached into my backpack. "I brought a pitch pipe."

Dev's head shot back. "Whoa." He ducked back down pretty quickly, though, when a kid tossed a drink into the garbage and sprayed droplets of icy soda everywhere.

After a minute, we'd figured out the notes: C-D-F-E-D-C. Dev twisted the dials. The lock opened right away. As before, we found a rolled-up slip of paper inside, covered in gold glitter. Underneath the sparkles we read the following scrawls:

40°
74°
Hamilton

"Forty, seventy-four, Hamilton?" I asked.

"What are those little circles?" Dev had to shout over the sounds of music now blaring from the karaoke speakers.

"Not sure." I stared at the paper. I started to twist a corkscrew curl around a finger but then released it and threw both my hands up. "They're coordinates!" I reached into my pocket and dug out the scrap of paper with Magpie's information. "And these marks on Magpie's note! They don't stand for feet. They're minutes."

Dev looked as confused as a little girl holding her hand between her legs who'd just come out of the men's room whimpering and looking from side to side.

"They're part of the address," I explained. "Remember? Mrs. Dearg was telling us about different ways to write coordinates with degrees, minutes, and seconds."

Dev grabbed the paper and stared at it. "Hmm." He held it next to Macaw's note. "Where do they point?"

I stared at the paper but felt as flustered as a tech-unsavvy hiker trying to decipher a navigation system manual. "Not sure."

When the loud speakers crackled to life, I gave up trying to concentrate. A scratchy voice blared, "Enter the raffle for a chance to win a monstrous, theater-sized, house-leveling flat-screen TV! Get your tickets before time runs out!"

Dev glanced at his watch "Oops. Our time's run out. My mom's coming back soon." He gestured toward the box. "Do we take this with us?"

"No." I rolled up the note and put it back in the compartment. Then I returned Macaw to the container and covered it with the log book.

"If we leave it here, Fife & Drum and Rather Be Fishing won't know we've seen it."

"Good idea."

Amid bleeps from machines and cries from kids whining about burst balloons we put the cache back exactly where we'd found it. We then headed toward the exit, trying not to step in spilled popcorn and other accidents on the way.

* * *

Dev's mom needed him to watch his little sister at home, so they dropped me off. I'd barely kicked off my shoes and grabbed a snack before he called me.

"So, where do the coordinates point?" he asked.

"Hold on a sec." I opened a map site on the Internet.

"What did Macaw say again? Forty, seventy-four?"

I found the scrap of paper with the coordinates. "Macaw says forty degrees on the top, and Magpie says forty-eight minutes. The second lines say seventy-four degrees and eighteen minutes."

Just as I entered the numbers, Marcus barged into my room. "I'm stuck!"

I stared at the screen, fixated on what would appear. Soon I sensed Marcus peering over my shoulder. "Get out of my room!"

He didn't budge.

"Hold on," I said to Dev. I blocked the screen with my arms. With my foot, I shooed Marcus toward the door.

"I need help." Marcus stood on his tiptoes and tried to peer around me at the screen. "And Mom's busy."

I grabbed his elbow and tugged him across the floor.

"I have to write a poem about animals," Marcus protested. "And I need a word that rhymes with snout."

"*Out* rhymes with snout," I said. "So get out of my room!" I dropped his arm and pointed toward the door. Slumping back down in my chair, I squinted at the screen.

Marcus soon made a reappearance at my side.

"What is wrong with you?" I covered the display with a notebook.

"It has to be about animals!" He peered over the notebook. "And rhyme with snout."

I gave up trying to hide the screen from Marcus as I, too, stared at the map on it. I scrolled down and scanned the markings, trying to recognize some landmark or body of water.

Nothing seemed even remotely familiar.

"What about *trout*?" Dev's voice sounded from the phone.

Oops. I'd left him hanging. "Trout? What?"

"Yeah, trout. I just saw something about trout sushi on a cooking show. Some celebrity in New York started serving it in his restaurant. Now it's a hit, and fishermen are all over the lakes in New Jersey, searching for the trout. But no one knows how he makes it. It tells in some book called *Guarded Recipes*, but you can't find it anywhere."

"*Trout, snout,*" Marcus said. "Yeah, that'll work! The grizzly caught a trout, then stuffed it in its snout." Still chanting, he bounced out of my room.

"So, back to business," Dev said. "What did you come up with?"

"Uh..." I stared at the hallway, open-mouthed, amazed at how easily Dev had gotten rid of Marcus. "Um..." I turned back to the screen and zoomed out several notches. "Kyrgyzstan. It points to Kyrgyzstan."

"Kyrgyzstan? You're making that up, right? Or Marcus messed with the coordinates."

"No, I'm serious." I checked the data again and scrolled out further. "It's somewhere near China."

"But what does that mean?"

"Not sure." I twisted a strand of hair. "But we don't have all the information yet. Rather Be Fishing still has Quail Box. He said he'd drop it off somewhere this weekend. Once we see what it's carrying, we'll know more."

"Right." Dev didn't sound entirely convinced. "Hey, there's a pitching clinic tonight at the rec center. You going?"

"A pitching clinic?"

"Yeah. I picked up a flyer at school. It says something about tips and drills, plus one-on-one contact with school coaches. We could use a break from the boxes. Want to check it out?"

I hated to abandon the mystery, even for one evening. But a trip to Kyrgyzstan wasn't happening anytime soon. "Sure. Maybe it'll help me make the softball team this spring."

"Great." Voices from Dev's TV suddenly blared, followed by yelps and a crash. "Oops. See you later."

CHAPTER 5

With the pitching clinic to look forward to, I zipped through my sax pieces and then plowed, full steam, into my homework. Worries kept pestering me, though: The quail box might end up far away, like in Kyrgyzstan. And why did Macaw's coordinates point there? If the boxes led to valuables, I needed to decode their message by yesterday. But how would I get halfway across the world?

In spite of my frazzled state, I wrapped up all my assignments. With my evening free for softball, I practically waltzed down to dinner. I stopped short, however, at my mom's response to my plans.

"I'm sorry, Erin, but I need you to stay home with Marcus tonight." She barely looked up as she dished out some microwaved frozen lasagna. "I have a meeting at work, and the sitter's not available."

"What?" I felt like a butterfly hit by a hailstone. Instead of pitching, I'd spend the evening losing at Resh-opoly.

"I'm so sorry, Erin." My mom shook her head. "There's nothing I can do."

When cooking timers, a boiling tea kettle, and the smoke alarm then sounded simultaneously, she sprang up to quell the commotion, and the conversation ended.

I left the table with a bitter taste in my mouth that had nothing to do with the radicchio in my ready-to-eat side salad. Back in my room, my chair scraped as I dragged it across the floor. I slumped down at my desk and yanked out my phone, feeling as tormented as the screaming baby in the next apartment. After punching random buttons for a while, I opened a text window.

> *Erin: Uncle El?*

I jabbed the sharp end of a bent paperclip into a notepad.

> *Erin: I need Dad now. If he was here, I wouldn't have to stay with Marcus tonight & I'd go to the clinic. How am I supposed to make the school team if I never practice?*

My fist banged down on the desk. Not allowing time for a response, I continued.

> *Erin: I need to solve the mystery before Rather Be Fishing or Fife & Drum do. If there's an opal in Kyrgyzstan, I need to find it now so I can see Dad.*

My fingers rapped my desk, and I felt my nostrils flaring as I stared at my phone. Uncle El had seen my texts. Why hadn't he answered? Even when I needed to talk in the middle of the night, he always got back to me immediately.

I clenched my fists and slammed my eyes shut. They grew moist anyway.

> *Erin: I wish Dad was here.*

My breath grew shallow, and my chest started shaking. But then a flash on the screen caught my attention.

Uncle El: Some music for you...

A snort burst from my nose. Probably the music was supposed to cheer me up. But I needed my dad, not therapeutic tunes.

I powered off the phone, cutting the session short. Resh-opoly might rank lower on the fun scale than a picnic in a hailstorm. In fact, I suspected Marcus had rigged it, because he always won. But at least no one would brainwash me into thinking things were fine.

* * *

I stared at my ginger tofu sandwich at lunch the next day. The wilted green stuff dangling out of it made me long for seventh grade, when the cafeteria still served chips, fries, and iced cupcakes. "Want to help me drop off Magpie this afternoon?" I asked Dev between difficult swallows.

"Sure. Faster than Resh can engage his electromagnetic shields, I'll be there." Dev took a bite of sandwich. Then he choked. "You're dropping off Magpie? Before you figure out what it means?" He sounded as indignant as if I'd tried to donate all of Marcus's Resh Renner spy gear to charity.

"Yeah, I need to. It's a trackable. It's not meant to be kept."

"But what if it leads to a precious opal? Or to a map showing the Seven Cities of Gold? Aren't you worried someone else might figure it out and beat you to the prize?"

"Yeah." I opened my carton of almond milk. "But first off, we don't know what's behind the message. It might only lead to a chest full of pirate patches and other junk left over from some kid's birthday party. Second, geocachers respect the rules. We take care of each other's caches and help each other's trackables along."

"Okay. I get it." Dev held up his palms to cut me off. "The longer people hang onto something, the sooner that sense of community falls apart. But still, what if Rather Be Fishing or Fife & Drum get hold of it?"

I bit my lip. "It's a risk we have to take. Besides, if Rather Be Fishing sees us playing by the rules, he might change his mind and tell us Quail's info."

Dev still looked scandalized.

I planted my elbows on the table. "Listen. The box needs to travel east, and I know of a mystery cache downtown that's east of here. It's called Steaming Cauldron, and it's the perfect place to leave the box. Chances are no one will pick it up again soon."

"What?" Dev flicked his straw wrapper into the air. "No one can crack its code?"

"Yeah. Only five people have ever found it. Its web page doesn't even give a location. It just lists some initial coordinates. You in?"

"Sure. Anything other than hanging out with my cousins." Dev wolfed down more grated ginger root. "Hey, speaking of remote places, when you entered the coordinates yesterday, you never gave any directions, did you? Like north, south, east, or west?"

"Um, I don't think so." I took a sip from my carton. My tongue drowned in almond slime.

"So the map assumed you meant forty degrees *north* and seventy-four degrees *east*, but it could have been forty *north* and seventy-four *west*."

I stopped chewing. "Or forty *south* and seventy-four *east* or *west*." I felt my eyes growing wide. "I wonder where that would put us?"

"Well..." Dev cleared his throat as if about to make an announcement. "I happened to do some research late last night." With a smug look, he pulled a slip of paper out of his pocket. "Forty south and seventy-four east lands us in the Indian Ocean. At forty south and seventy-four west, we're in the Pacific Ocean, just off the western coast of Chile. And forty north and seventy-four west puts us in the Atlantic Ocean, right off the coast of New Jersey."

"Not that far from here." Without thinking, I gulped my milk.

"So, basically, if we rent a submarine, we can check out three of the four locations."

I ignored his quip. "Maybe it's an extreme cache—one that's impossible to reach, unless you've got scuba gear or a rock-climbing harness or a space shuttle."

"In that case, we can be thankful the coordinates are somewhere on earth."

"Right, but don't forget Quail Box probably has the third part of the coordinates. Once we have the complete address, the location may shift." I poked at the squishy white chunks in my sandwich. "If only Rather Be Fishing would let us see Quail Box, we'd be set."

"He probably discovered its hidden message and knows it leads to something valuable, like a massive opal, and doesn't want to share the info."

* * *

We headed to Steaming Cauldron that afternoon. At first it looked like the easiest cache ever. The initial coordinates led us to some prickly bushes near a strip mall, where we found a film canister. Our problems started once we opened it, though.

Inside we found a picture of a cauldron, but nothing else, not even coordinates. We scratched our heads and looked around for big, black, bubbling kettles. Then everything got really hairy.

"Erin?" Dev asked. "See that woman over there?" He pointed toward the shops. Someone with ridiculously long, blond curls had just left a music store and was headed in our direction.

"She looks just like the baby-sitter from the park, Fife & Drum."

"Exactly."

She shot several glances in our direction as she got into a car. Then she pulled out of the lot, but things only got worse.

"Look at that magnet on her car." Dev pointed to her back bumper.

"'Drummers live longer, 'cause they keep time,'" I read.

"Basically it proves she's Fife & Drum, doesn't it?"

"Yeah. And that's bad news. She's already had Quail Box and Macaw. Now she must be after Magpie, too."

"We'd better find that cache and get out of here before someone sees us with it."

I poked around some milk cartons on the side of the strip mall.

"Look, a cauldron!" Dev called out from the front of a candy store. Surrounded by gargoyles and Venus Flytraps, it stood in a flower box near the store's entrance.

We brushed through leaves and cobwebs inside it until we found a plastic container. Judging by the impressive collection of cheap party favors it held, we had definitely located the cache.

I signed the log while Dev deposited Magpie. Then I opened a bottle of bubbles someone had left in the cache. To celebrate our find, I blew a stream in Dev's direction. Somehow I also managed to spill half the bottle on Dev.

His jaw dropped when he saw the huge wet spot on his jeans. He grabbed the bubbles from me. I sprang back before he could launch a counterattack. But instead of showering me with the soapy slime, he replaced the cap and pocketed the bottle. "Just wait," he said with an evil smile. "I'll get my revenge."

I kept my distance as we walked back to our bikes. I felt bad about Dev's wet, goopy jeans. To make him feel better, I didn't head in the other direction when I saw an ad for the new Resh movie. "Look," I said instead. It hung outside a cinema next to the music shop.

"It's playing this weekend!" Dev announced.

I started to cower over his enthusiasm but then stopped. I used to love watching the teenage spy. Plus, going to the movies would beat doing the laundry or whatever other exciting plans Mom had scheduled for me.

Dev checked the play times. "I've got to watch my little sister today, but it's showing tomorrow afternoon. Want to go?"

"Sure." Just to make Dev's day, I added, "Faster than Resh can eliminate a contingent of death 'droids, I'll be there."

Chapter 6

Later, I logged our visit to Steaming Cauldron at Geocaching.com and entered Magpie's new location. I also visited Quail Box's page. We'd managed to drop off Magpie and escape Fife & Drum, but we'd moved no closer to getting hold of Quail and pinpointing the exact location of the boxes' coordinates.

None of the links offered any new information, though. Rather Be Fishing's post, about dropping off the box on his next trip, still leered out at me from the online log.

I only finished half my lunch the next day—Saturday. Mom sat with me at the kitchen table, partially hidden by a tall stack of presents she'd bought in bulk, but I barely heard her rambling on about birthday parties. Worry obsessed me. Where would Quail Box end up? And why had I ever agreed to go to the Resh movie? All the school bullies, like Pierce, the bulky chess team captain, would have a field day if someone saw Dev and me there. Mom got up and rummaged around a counter littered with gift wrap, cards, and ribbon, but her questions about who'd taken the tape went unanswered as I slunk out the front door, wishing I'd come down with the flu and could cancel.

As Dev's mom dropped us off in pouring rain, I smiled. The ticket line stretched around the corner of the building. In other words, we had no chance of getting in. Dev wanted to try anyway, though. He looked like he'd witnessed Resh's death. I pulled up my hood to disguise myself as we joined the end of the queue.

Before long, the line moved along, and against my wishes, we got tickets. I consoled myself with some popcorn.

The movie lasted more than two hours. Somehow, though, I didn't mind. Packed with extreme stunts, impossible getaways, and crowd-pleasing heroic deeds, it reminded me of grade school days, when Marcus, Dad, and I would watch Resh on TV.

Dev couldn't get enough of it. As we left the cinema, he danced around while whistling the theme song and then went into a play-by-play of Resh's hiccup move, in which he released a poison-tipped dart with only the slightest of abdominal twitches.

I tightened my hood even though the rain had stopped. "Well, what next?" I asked as we reached the street.

Dev looked at his watch and moaned. "My mom wants me home soon. I've got to stay in tonight with my sister while she and my dad go to a reception for my uncle. They'll be at some gala for my cousin all afternoon, but you said your mom could drive us home, right?"

"Uh..." My face grew hot, and not just from my hood. "She said she could at first, but she might be busy taking my brother to a party now." I fumbled in my pocket for my phone.

"No, I can't pick you up right now." Mom's annoyed voice rang out from the other end of the line. "I explained that earlier, Erin. Marcus's ride to the robot party fell through, so I'm with him now at Kidz Labz. At 4:45 we go straight to the Science Center for a lightning party at five. I doubt we'll be home before seven."

"Bummer." I stuffed the phone back into my pocket. "My mom can't drive right now." I kicked at a rock in the street. "When are you supposed to be home?"

"Around five thirty."

I tilted my head from side to side and sucked in a breath. "We might make it if we hurry a little."

"We could cut through the park by the lake."

"Sure, if you think it'll save time." I looked down the street in the direction of the park. Then I felt my eyes grow wide. "Actually, that's a great idea."

Dev stopped mimicking Resh's hiccup maneuver for a second and looked over. "What do you mean?"

"I think Rather Be Fishing lives in the neighborhood by the lake."

"Really?"

"Yeah. I remember him saying something at that geocaching event about being close to the lake and the good fishing."

Dev gulped. "You mean Quail Box could be in one of these houses?"

"Exactly."

"But how will we figure out which one?"

I bit my lip and crossed my arms. Then I threw my hands up. "He drives a bright red pickup. I remember seeing it at the event."

* * *

We combed the lake neighborhood for the next hour, checking every driveway and open garage for a red truck.

After reaching the end of yet another street without any luck, Dev took a seat on the curb.

I sat down, too, and twisted a strand of hair. "We've got to find it. Otherwise, Quail will end up far in the West tomorrow."

	Quail	Magpie	Macaw
Fife-And-Drum	Moved it out of the woods.	Hasn't seen it.	Moved it from History-Geeks-Delight to Karaoke-Candy.
Rather-Be-Fishing	Has it right now. Promised to drop it off on fishing trip this weekend.	Hasn't seen it.	Moved it out of the woods.
Water-Break (me)	Waiting for Rather-BeFishing to drop it off.	Moved it from woods to Steaming-Cauldron.	Saw it in Karaoke-Candy.

"Like in the Pacific. Or hidden under jagged rocks in a riverbed, guarded twenty-four/seven by piranhas."

I slumped. "And someone else will pick it up before we can get out there."

"Yeah, like Fife & Drum."

"No. Fife & Drum's already had Quail." I pulled a sheet of paper out of my pocket.

"What's that?"

I started to unfold it but then stopped. "It's nothing." I folded it back up.

Dev shot me a sideways, skeptical glance. Then he snagged the paper out of my hands. I tried to grab it back, but he twisted around, blocking me. I reached around him, but he'd already unfolded it and scanned it over.

"Nothing, huh? It kind of looks like one of Mrs. Dearg's assignments."

"I... uh..." Yes, the idea had come from Mrs. Dearg. I guess she'd ingrained rubrics a little too deeply in our heads because I'd set up a table for the boxes. "I just thought it might help us keep track of everything."

"Of course." Dev relished the moment, flashing a victorious smile.

I pointed to Fife & Drum's row to change the subject. "See? Fife & Drum's the one who moved Quail out of the woods."

Dev studied the sheet. "What's to stop her from getting it again and keeping it from us?" He crumpled the paper and tossed it over his shoulder.

I didn't have a good answer, but I picked up the sheet and pocketed it as another question came to mind. "Hey, wasn't Mrs. Dearg talking about a fife and drum corps the other day?" Forgetting our futile search, we both laughed at the thought of our history teacher and her agendas, procedures, and checklists. Her '80s fashions also fueled the conversation. When Dev started going on about her neon-colored leg warmers and the shoulder pads in her blazers, we nearly rolled into the street in a giggle fit. Finally I stood up.

"Come on, just a few more streets." I tugged on Dev's wrist and led the way around the corner.

I sped up when something red caught my eye at the far end of the next street.

Dev must have seen it, too, because he set off at a sprint.

I squinted as I ran to catch up. It looked like a red truck, parked at the curb.

Dev slowed down as he approached it. Then he stopped short, stared at the truck for a second, and bolted back toward me.

"It's definitely his truck." Dev paused to catch his breath. "See that sticker on the back?"

As I looked, sunlight lit up a brightly colored magnet on the pickup's bumper.

"It's Rather Be Fishing's signature." Dev reached into his pocket and pulled out the coin he'd picked up geocaching the previous weekend. "Same design."

Turning back to the pickup, we crept along a row of hedges on the edge of the yard and peered through the branches.

A driveway split the front yard, leading from the street up to the garage. Behind the house, a back door led onto a small patio and lawn. At the back of the yard stood a garden shed with its doors wide open.

"This must be his house," Dev whispered. "Look at all the fishing gear back there." He pointed to a collection of poles lined up just inside the shed door.

Suddenly the screen door in the back swung open with

a creak. A heavyset man emerged from the house, whistling, and lumbered over to the shed.

We watched through the bushes as he rummaged through fishing supplies.

"It looks like he's leaving soon." I peered around the shrubs to get a better look. "He said in the e-mail that he'd drop off Quail on a fishing trip tomorrow."

"Maybe the box is in the shed, too. Should we ask him about it?"

"I don't know. He said he wouldn't give it to us directly."

Without warning, a scratchy voice then rang out from the house. "Harold?"

Dev and I dived down behind the shrubs.

"Harold?" the voice screeched. "You promised to replace that light bulb in the bathroom. And while you're at it, the sink in there is stopped up again."

Harold let out a loud sigh.

"It doesn't sound like he's in a good mood," Dev said.

"Yeah. I'm not sure we can convince him to show us Quail."

A minute later Harold trudged through the wet yard to the house. After the screen door slammed shut, Dev and I stared at each other.

Dev shrugged. "We could just take a look in the shed."

I twisted a strand of hair. "I'm not so sure that's a good idea."

"What about the clues, though? Don't you want to solve this mystery?"

"Of course I do, but—"

"We're so close. Come on. Just one quick peek won't hurt."

Dev had a point. And if the box was with the fishing gear just inside the door, we wouldn't even have to set foot inside the shed. "Okay. But let's make it fast."

Tiptoeing, we entered the backyard and approached the small building. Harold's wife would probably keep him busy in the house for a while. Still, we felt exposed out in the open, so we cowered just inside the shed door.

I sifted through some nets. Dev inspected other gear. He had just moved aside a rod when a creak startled us. The house's screen door had swung open. Harold then stepped out onto the wet patio.

I looked around but saw no way out.

Harold let the door slam and then plodded through huge puddles that had pooled on the concrete. Like a tank on the march, he was advancing toward us.

With nowhere else to go, I darted behind a wheelbarrow leaning against the back wall of the shed, half buried underneath a pile of rags. Dev scrambled under a tarp draped over the edge of a shelf.

Harold sloshed through the waterlogged yard and reached the shed.

Dev and I held our breath as he poked through his fishing gear.

"Ah, here it is," Harold mumbled after a minute. "Must've dropped it earlier." We then heard a squish as he stepped back into the wet grass.

Still barely breathing, we crouched, helplessly still, as Harold closed the doors, throwing us into darkness. Next, we heard a click followed by more sloshes that grew ever fainter, as Harold's boots tramped back through the puddles toward the house.

Curled up in my hiding place, I felt my heart hammering, just like the fast, ringing percussion in the Resh movie during suspenseful scenes. Adding to the tense mood, a few shafts of fading afternoon sunlight filtered through gaps in the shed's walls but provided little light. A moldy, musty smell also filled the air. Honestly, though, I didn't care. Only one thought occupied my head.

"That was close," Dev whispered.

"Right. And I don't think it's over yet. I'm pretty sure he padlocked the shed."

* * *

"He locked it?" Dev's voice shook. Next I heard the tarp rustling. Then I heard, "Ow!" as Dev scuffled across the plywood floor toward the door. He banged into it a few times but soon gave up.

My heart beat wildly all over again, like the tom-toms in the movie's breathtaking scenes. I made my way out from behind the wheelbarrow and over to the door. I rammed against it with my shoulders, but nothing budged.

I took a deep breath. "Um... it looks like we're locked inside."

"Right. That pretty much sums it up."

"Okay." I held up my hands. "Let's look at our options."

"Wait." Dev groped around in the dark. "I think I saw a flashlight in here somewhere. On the shelf maybe." He explored further. "Let's at least try to find it first if we're holding a meeting. It might shed some light on the situation. Heh, heh."

How Dev could find humor at this time, I couldn't fathom.

"Here it is." Dev switched on the light. He pointed it upward, casting the entire space in a dim glow. "The meeting can proceed."

"Okay." My voice sounded raspy. I cleared my throat. "The only obvious way out of here is the door, which we've already tried." I edged over to the wall and inspected the panels. "I suppose we could take this thing apart from the inside. There seem to be enough tools in here to do the job."

"And have the roof fall in on us?.On a scale from one to ten, I'd rate that a negative three."

"Right, not an ideal plan." I explored around in the weak light. "There's a sledgehammer in the corner. We could smash a hole in the back wall."

"We'd make a racket in the process, though. We'd probably get caught."

"True. Then we'd be in trouble for breaking in and also for the damage."

"Exactly. If the last idea got a negative three, this one gets a negative eight. I can think of better ways of spending my weekends than doing community service at the library."

I sighed as I reached for my phone. "We could call my mom, explain everything, and have her come get us."

"Not good." Dev shook his head. "Still negative. We'd be in trouble with our parents and also with Harold-Who'd-Rather-Be-Fishing."

"But what's the alternative?" My voice came out high and squeaky, like I'd gulped air from a party balloon. I tried to steel myself. "I suppose we could wait here until morning, when Harold loads the fishing gear into the truck. We'd still be in big trouble, but at least there'd be no damage."

"Uh ... negative five on my scale. We'd have to spend a cold night in here with the spiders." Dev batted at cobwebs on his jeans. "Our parents would call the police sometime this evening to report us missing. Sounds like double the trouble with only mediocre accommodations."

I watched as Dev picked up a nail from a tin on a shelf and chucked it at something chirping away near the door.

"Unless you'd like cricket for breakfast," he said.

I glanced around and inched away from the wall. "Calling my mom is looking like a pretty good idea. She's not home yet, though. We'll have to wait at least another hour."

"All right. That's the plan. Meeting adjourned." Dev surveyed the back wall. "As long as we're stuck here, I'll see if we can remove just a few of the back panels without toppling the entire thing. Or maybe we could take the door off its hinges."

Dev turned around to study it.

"Good idea. I'll try to find Quail Box in the meantime."

"Not sure what good it'll do us if we die of venom poisoning before we can use the information." Dev swatted at something on his arm. "But I guess it couldn't hurt."

I checked the fishing gear near the door. As I opened a tackle box, the tom-toms inside me thumped wildly again but this time to a happier beat. Right on top sat a small wooden box. Its lid pictured a grayish bird with a funny-looking knot sticking out of its head.

Did quails' heads have weird bumps on them? I turned the box over, checking the bottom for a sliding panel. A gasp escaped my throat as it slid open. "I've got it! I found Quail Box! Now I just need to crack the lock."

I opened the box's lid and let it play. The notes rang out through the air about as loudly as a fire alarm. I grabbed the tarp Dev had hidden underneath and wound it around the box to muffle the sound. "Sorry about that. I need to listen a few times to figure out the notes."

"No problem." Dev sifted through a toolbox and pulled out a screw driver that seemed to satisfy him. "The police sirens will soon drown it out when we're discovered."

I raised my eyebrows at Dev's comment. Then I doubly wrapped the box with the tarp, leaving only the top free. Figuring out the pitches would be tricky, here in a creepy shed with no saxophone. Still, I opened the box and let it play again.

The tune started low and then went up in pitch, ending on a high note.

I tried humming it. Not sure of the first note, I listened once more, committing everything to memory this time.

The flashlight flickered, distracting me. I looked up at the cracks below the roof, now dim. The sun must have set. If the flashlight went out, we'd be stuck in complete darkness.

A shudder rocked my frame. My breathing grew shallow until I realized the lack of light might help me focus on the music, the same way blind people often made good musicians.

I handed the flashlight to Dev. "Here. Take this. You'll have more luck with a direct beam."

When Dev didn't object, I focused on the first two pitches. Having practiced countless scales on my horn, I realized they were only a half step apart, like E and F. I hummed some more. "Then it goes one step higher to G then back to F."

"Look at this!" Dev combed through a shelf. "Garden gnomes. A whole collection. That guy could open up a museum of tacky yard art."

I ignored him as I hummed another scale and found something that sounded like the box's fifth pitch, a C. The sixth note was then only a step higher, at D.

I moved back toward Dev and the light. He was pushing on a gnome's hat and then watching as it dropped its pants in response. After unwinding the tarp from the wooden box, I twisted the lock's dials, aligning them with the notes I'd found. I sucked in my breath and pulled on the latch.

It held fast.

Suppressing a groan, I shook it and then checked the dials and tried the latch again.

Nothing clicked.

Chapter 7

The air had grown colder. My stomach grumbled, and my throat felt dry, reminding me of geocaching in the desert, something my family had once attempted while vacationing in southern Arizona. With the humidity level at a record low, we'd been forced to turn back halfway into our trek. We'd run out of water. Also, orange slices we'd packed for the hike had shriveled into prune-like clumps.

In spite of everything, I turned back to the box. Where had I gone wrong? My fingers twisted knots in my curls as I checked the notes again. The intervals seemed right, but maybe the tune didn't begin on E. Was there another spot on the scale with only a half step between notes?

I stretched my legs, which had fallen asleep, and hummed a scale. The last two notes, B and C, seemed close in pitch. I closed my eyes in concentration. Then, while Dev reported on more gnomes he'd found, including some scratching embarrassing itches and others looking drunk, I transposed everything to start on B. Finally I grabbed the box and set the dials to the new sequence, B-C-D-C-G-A.

My fingers now numb with cold, I fumbled with some of the letters. The flashlight's faint beam didn't help.

Suddenly I drew a sharp intake of frosty air. The latch had released.

The bottom opened, revealing a familiar-looking, tattered, rolled-up scrap of paper. Snatching the note from the box, I unrolled it and wiped a layer of glitter off its surface. "Fifty-eight, *N*, fifty-nine—"

"Shhhh!" Dev cut me off, mid-sentence. "Someone's coming!"

I glanced at the paper in my hand for one final split second before shoving it back in the hidden compartment. With no time to think, I dived behind the wheelbarrow, tucking in my head and limbs. I heard Dev rustling with the tarp as heavy footsteps approached the shed.

Next, as someone outside fiddled with the padlock, I gasped. Quail Box was still in my hand. Even worse, the lid of the tackle box lay wide open, right inside the shed door.

"Wrong key." The voice came from just outside the shed. The sound of jingling metal then filled the air.

Afraid a better opportunity would never come along, I sprang out from behind the wheelbarrow and lunged toward the door. Hearing Harold still rummaging with the keys, I placed Quail Box in the tackle box and shut its lid. Just as the fiddling stopped, I darted back behind the wheelbarrow, scraping my knee on the way. Not daring to breathe, I clutched my throbbing leg and pulled some rags back over the wheelbarrow as the door opened.

"'Church rummage sale,' said the lady." We heard Harold's tired voice in the dark. "Wants me to haul all this old stuff out of here. And where has she left that flashlight now? Never putting things back where they belong."

Harold made shuffling sounds. Afraid the top of my head was visible over the edge of the wheelbarrow, I inched down lower.

"So much stuff," Harold muttered. "Maybe I should use the wheelbarrow."

My heart stopped, as if the movie music conductor had silenced the orchestra, mid-recording.

More scuffles followed as Harold stepped across the plywood. "Would save me a few trips."

I held my breath and twisted curls around fingers on both my hands, sure this dicey game of hide-and-seek was about to end in a bad way. Then I released my hair as an idea popped into my head. Keeping my fingers hidden under an oily rag, I grasped the wheelbarrow handles in a tight grip.

Harold must have grabbed hold of the other end because I felt a tug. He yanked again, trying to jerk the wheelbarrow in the opposite direction, but I held on. The square handles were probably leaving permanent creases in my fingers, along with a few splinters, but I didn't let the wheelbarrow budge.

Harold gave it one more tug. "Ah! It's not worth the trouble." He released it. "Can't get it free. It must be caught on the shelf." He must have found the flashlight because a faint beam of light appeared. It flickered as he aimed it at the shelf holding the garden figures, where Dev was hiding.

Harold then began shuffling back and forth. Several times he brushed against the tarp. Just when I thought he might knock it loose and expose Dev, he scuffled toward the door.

Squish. He stepped into the wet grass. More splashes followed. I peeked out from my cover. He'd lumbered off into the yard, his arms full with gnomes.

Once he was out of earshot, I scrambled out from the wheelbarrow. "Come on! Let's get out of here while we can!"

"Yeah. Before he comes back for the pair of mating

gnomes." Dev disentangled himself from the tarp and stepped onto the wet grass. A fence enclosed the entire back lawn. "Where to? He'll spot us in the yard."

"Back here!" I pointed behind the shed.

Faster, Dev would say, than Resh Renner's hover-mobile in warp speed, we darted behind the small building, hurdling a thorny bush on the way. Pressing our backs to the shed's rear wall, we panted, catching our breath.

"I don't care if we're standing in poison oak–infested quicksand," Dev said. "I'm so glad to be out of that shed." When a squishing sound returned, as Harold made his way back across the wet grass, he and I shushed our breathing and then waited, wide-eyed.

First we heard Harold knocking stuff around, but then his movements stopped. For what seemed like eons, he stood completely still. Maybe we'd left something behind. Or maybe the pants on that one gnome were stuck in the dropped position. For the umpteenth time that afternoon, the drums in my heart pounded furiously.

At long last, we heard Harold rounding up more gnomes. Next, the padlock clicked shut, and his boots splashed across the yard toward the garage.

"I think he's inside now." I peeked around the side of the shed.

"Let's make a run for it before his wife decides the hedges need trimming or the fence needs whitewashing!"

Dev and I squeezed under the fence into the adjoining backyard. We crept along the row of hedges. At last we made it to the street and set off at a sprint. My thighs burned as intensely as if I'd just hiked fifty switchbacks up the face of a mountain. Neither of us stopped, though, until we'd reached the far side of the next neighborhood.

* * *

Panting, I caught up to the long-legged, athletic Dev, who had sprung ahead in our escape. "Help me. Remember. Something!" I sputtered between gasps of cold air. "Fifty-eight. *N*. Fifty-nine. *W*. *B*!"

"Fifty-eight, *N*, fifty-nine, *W*, *B*?" Dev looked up from the curb where he sat, recovering.

"It was on the note inside Quail Box." I stopped to catch my breath. "I think there were quotes after the numbers, which stand for minutes, or parts of degrees. It must be the final piece of the coordinates."

"And what's the *B*?"

"No idea. Once we get back, we'll put everything together and try to figure it out."

"Speaking of getting back, what time is it?"

My jaw nearly dropped to the ground with my tired legs as I glanced at my watch. The hour read eight. I didn't bother looking at the minutes.

Picking up the pace again, we jogged through a few more neighborhoods. Then we split up, each heading home.

Mom didn't exactly backflip with joy over my late arrival. In fact, she grounded me. She also banned the TV, my phone, and the Internet for a week. In other words, I finally had the complete geographic coordinates but had no way to look up where they pointed to.

Back in school the next Monday, Dev immediately dismissed my tech restrictions as mild. "Before I even got both feet through the front door, my mom pulled the plug on the Internet. She and my dad were really late to their dinner because I wasn't there to baby-sit. So now they're making me watch my little sister every day after school until fall break."

"When does break start?"

"A week from Thursday," Dev answered as we reached our lockers. "I have to baby-sit for ten days straight. Hey, what about the coordinates? Did you figure out where they lead?"

"Nope. I checked a globe but couldn't zero in on the exact spot."

"Still somewhere in Kyrgyzstan?"

"Not even close. It's somewhere in New Jersey." I pulled a slip of paper out of my pocket. "Take a look."

Scrawled on the already dog-eared sheet was the following information:

40° 48' 58" N
74° 18' 59" W
Hamilton, Opal B.

"If we could only get on the Internet, we'd know for sure."

Just to make our mouths water, a kid holding a phone walked by, even though school policy banned cells. My eyes latched onto his screen, aglow with a web page. The opportunity vanished when he turned into a stairwell, but some straight-haired girls then appeared around the corner, giggling and also punching keys on phones.

I could ask to borrow one. But they were talking about lip gloss shades and emergency trips to the tanning salon. And a few wore magenta mascara.

No, I couldn't ask them. Their circus clown makeup made me gag. Plus, they'd all covered their cells in sparkly cases, and a few were drooling over Pierce, the massive chess team captain.

"Erin? Hello?" I spun around at Dev's voice and ended up slamming my locker door on my finger.

"What?"

"The library!" Dev sounded as excited as if Resh Renner had personally answered his fan mail.

"What about it?" I sucked on my throbbing finger.

"We can plug the coordinates into a computer at the Northlawn Library."

"Oh, yeah! Great idea." I gave Dev a high-five for saving me from the glitter girls.

That night, though, my mom had a different opinion. "You're grounded," she reminded me. "No trips anywhere. Not even the library."

Dev's parents told him pretty much the same thing.

The next few days, thoughts of Fife & Drum and Rather Be Fishing made my stomach churn. They'd probably both picked up all three boxes, but I couldn't go online to check. Making things worse, I ran into girls with smuggled, flashy phones at every turn. Then Dev remembered the school library.

"History's meeting in the media center today!" he said, as he pulled some wadded up gym clothes out of his backpack.

"So? What's so exciting about research skills?"

"The coordinates!" Dev dug further in his pack, this time finding a science project involving chicken skin. "We can plug them in!"

"But those computers are off limits." I didn't feel like getting in more trouble, especially while still serving a sentence for my last crime.

Dev shrugged. "I'll create a distraction."

"No." I handed him a dog-eared binder he'd dropped. "I've got a better idea."

History started, and Ms. Mode, the school librarian, brushed a piece of lint off her custom-made Italian blazer.

"Hernan Cortes, class. I'd like you to research five facts on Cortes's schemes to appropriate Aztec gold."

Amid groans and eye rolls, the class dispersed.

"Can I look something up on the Internet?" I asked Ms. Mode.

She adjusted her postmodern Danish eyewear. "Is it related to Hernan Cortes?"

I looked her in the eye and put on my most modest smile. "No."

Frowning, Ms. Mode scrutinized me. She looked as annoyed as if she'd walked through a woods on a spring day and had run into inchworm silk with every step. Finally she lifted her nose and sniffled sharply. "One minute. You get one minute on the Internet."

I ran over to a computer. Meanwhile, Dev engaged Ms. Mode in a conversation about lake trout sushi, to buy me some time.

A little later, we met up behind a bookshelf. "So you follow the tabloid gossip?" I couldn't resist poking fun at him.

"Give me a break." Dev swatted the air with his hand. "I've seen the same magazines on Ms. Mode's desk that my mom has at home and happen to know that *Guarded Recipes* is the hottest thing to hit the forty-something female crowd lately."

Before I could make fun of Dev's apparent in-depth knowledge of fads hitting older women's circles, he got back to business. "So, what did you dig up?"

"The library," I said.

"The library? We're in the library. What do you mean?"

"Not this one. The Northlawn Library. The coordinates point to the library here in town."

"But that doesn't make sense. You don't think an opal's buried there, do you? Or is this some booklover's idea of a joke?" His tone turned mockingly serious. "Knowledge is treasure. Visit the library."

"No idea. Maybe it's just a rare copy of *Guarded Recipes*. But I still think it's worth checking out."

* * *

From its perch among stacks of books and papers on my desk, my computer pleaded with me to power it on that evening. Its telltale welcome beeps would alert my mom, though. She'd probably extend the Internet ban. Still, I ached to log into Geocaching.com to see what had become of the wooden boxes. For all I knew, the feds had already picked up all three, deciphered the coordinates, and conducted an extensive search of the Northlawn Library, leaving nothing but overturned book carts and faded, ransacked card catalog files in their wake.

Finally I begged Mom to let me go to the library after school the next day. Some kids considered reading a punishment, after all.

"Fine," she said, looking up from her screen. "But while you're downtown, you can swing by the farmer's market and pick up some apples. A dozen green ones. And watch out for traffic, especially by the lake. I've seen lots of pickups loaded with fishing gear racing out of there lately."

The idea of running errands didn't thrill me. Desperate for a chance to get out, though, I agreed.

The next afternoon, I found myself on the library's grounds. I'd visited the building before but had never paid the exterior any attention. Its deteriorating state now glared out at me. Towers, graceful stone archways, or gargoyles might have convinced me it hid a secret or maybe treasure. Instead, the dilapidated rectangular building I faced left me wondering whether it even offered any interesting books.

I headed toward the entrance anyway. The coordinates had pointed directly at the building. A pair of doors led inside, lined on either side by shrubs and leafy plants. I bent over and sifted through a bed of ground cover.

"Did you lose your homework in the bushes?" a kid yelled out as he walked by.

"No, she lost her lunch money," his friend said.

When another kid shouted, "You know, there's a girls' room right inside the door," I circled around the building to the back.

Small shrubs lined the foundation. I poked through the bushes, but when a scowling librarian came out for a cigarette break, I gave up and headed home. Halfway there, I stopped in my tracks. Mom had asked me to go to the farmer's market. I turned around and trudged back downtown.

Never having shopped at the Northlawn market, I expected to find two or three stands with homemade signs advertising apples and pumpkins. Instead, a maze of booths and vendors greeted me, offering everything from oven-hot bread and fresh sushi to stinky European cheeses.

I squeezed my way past a crowd of canvas-bag-toting bargain-hunters toward a produce stand and filled a sack with Granny Smiths. Just when I got in line to pay, a familiar, whiny voice made me look up in surprise and drop an apple. Behind the booth, near the back of a truck, stood Rather Be Fishing. A man in a smudged apron stood next to him.

Ducking down, I took a long time to pick up the stray apple while I listened in on their conversation.

"I'm sorry," the man in the bloodstained apron said. "But if you don't have it by next week, the deal is off."

"You've got to give me a few more weeks," Harold begged in his tired voice.

"I'm running out of time and patience." The vendor closed the truck's doors. "You've failed me a few times now. Next week, or you're out."

Although Harold let out another whine, the vendor waved him away and returned to his booth.

The next day at school, I filled Dev in on everything.

"It sounds like the other guy is paying Harold to deliver something." Dev leaned over and peered underneath a bench. He wanted to find a cache hidden on the school grounds, so we'd eaten lunch at the picnic tables. "Uh-oh. Do you think Harold figured out the coordinates, too?"

"I don't know. Maybe." I inspected a trash can. "He's had Macaw and Quail, but I can't tell if he's seen Magpie since I still can't get on my computer."

"Me neither." Dev stopped poking through the Dumpster when Ms. Mode crossed the parking lot and nearly tripped in her five-inch Belgian heels. "But if he did, it sounds like something valuable is hidden at the library. Maybe the other guy is paying him to track it down."

"Right." I fanned my nose when a breeze picked up and Dumpster fragrances wafted in my direction.

"What about Fife & Drum. Any chance she knows about the library?"

"Same scenario as Harold. She's seen Quail and Macaw but hopefully not Magpie, although we can't tell for sure."

Dev shook his head. "Somehow, we've got to get to the library before the others do."

"That place is packed every afternoon, though."

Dev scanned the outside of the Dumpster. "Maybe we could head over there at night, when no one's around."

I shot him my best skeptical look. "Will your parents let you out?"

"Next Wednesday they will, the first night of fall break. We could watch some movies, then slip out of the house."

"Seems like a long time to wait." I joined Dev at the Dumpster and tugged on a screw sticking out near the top. It came off easily. It also came apart when I twisted the top.

Dev took it and pulled a tightly wound paper log out of the inside. "Maybe we could do it tonight if I agree to an extra week of baby-sitting."

"Ooh. Would you do that?"

Dev signed the cache as the bell rang and Ms. Mode walked by, this time sporting nonskid Alaskan mukluks. "If you'll take half my shifts, I will."

* * *

Dev's parents rejected his offer. Worse, they extended his baby-sitting duties simply because he'd suggested the idea. They also starting keeping such close tabs on him that he didn't dare sneak out. However, they did agree to a movie night on the start of fall break. Still, we would have to wait nearly a week to search the library.

On Saturday, the phone woke me up.

"So what's the status on the boxes?" Dev asked from the other end.

"What?" I rubbed my eyes and yawned.

"You can go on the Internet now, right? Wasn't your mom lifting the ban today?"

"Oh, yeah." I switched on my computer. As it powered

up, yelps and cries shrilled at Dev's house. "Okay, I'm on Geocaching.com. Rather Be Fishing put Quail Box in a cache in western New Jersey last Sunday."

"Just like he promised."

"Right." I scrolled down. "Oh, no. He also found Steaming Cauldron this past week. His log says, 'Finally figured this one out.'"

"Did he take Magpie?"

"No." I clicked on Magpie's link. "But Fife & Drum did. She also found Steaming Cauldron the same day. And her log says, 'Found this one on the way to winning the big prize.'"

"'Big prize' doesn't sound good." Squeals and screams sounded from Dev's end. "But that's interesting about Rather Be Fishing. Maybe he got to the cache after Fife & Drum—too late to get Magpie. Or maybe he's on to the messages in the boxes, like we are, but doesn't want anyone to know he is. So he left the box in the cache to avoid leaving a trail."

"Yeah," I shouted back over some roars and barks. "Like we did with Macaw in Karaoke Candy." I tried to tell Dev that Macaw had reached the Caribbean in a geocaching race, but I gave up when he yelled something at his sister about eating outside, naked, to minimize the mess.

That evening, the phone rang again. I picked it up. "Hello?"

"Hey, Erin."

"Dad!" My eyes bulged. They probably looked like the pop-out facial features of a squeeze toy someone had stepped on, but I didn't care. "You'll never believe what I found geocaching!"

But before I could say any more, Marcus grabbed another phone. "Dad! A kid in my class tried trout sushi from *Guarded Recipes* in New York!"

"Yum."

"No, it was gross!" Marcus explained. "Who wants to eat raw fish? It has germs and parasites." A minute later, with Marcus still ranting about tapeworms and neurotoxins, I gave up on the conversation.

From my room I couldn't help noticing that Mom also barely said anything on the phone. I needed to do something—like buy Mom a ticket to Hawaii, so she and Dad could patch things up—before they decided to split for good.

Finally, the Wednesday before our two-day fall break arrived. Dev came over that evening. His parents probably would have made us baby-sit if we'd gone to the Johar house.

First we played video games. But after what seemed like mere minutes, my mom pulled the plug, claiming our eyes had glazed over and our brains had liquefied and oozed out our ears. I did notice my thumb twitching involuntarily as we put away the handsets. Then we crashed on the couch to watch *Thirteen Dead Bodies*. We hoped the movie's gore would drive the others away.

The plan worked well. Thirty minutes into it, the fifth corpse appeared.

"I've had enough," Mom said from the kitchen. She headed upstairs, taking Marcus with her.

Dev and I worked our way down the staircase leading to the back door, avoiding the creaky steps and floorboards. Silently, we edged open the sliding door leading outside and then set out into the night.

Chapter 8

The cold air whipped across my face, nipping at my nose and ears. Before long, though, we reached the library. A single street lamp cast a dim circle of light on the far end of the parking lot.

"What exactly are we looking for? An opal somewhere in this gravel?" Dev kicked at some pebbles in the path. "Or maybe in this pile of leaves?"

"No, something bigger." I switched on my flashlight. "An outside cellar door or a pile of freshly dug dirt. Or better yet, a trapdoor leading underground. Basically any place you could hide something." I checked my navigation app. "The arrow's pointing toward the entrance. Let's go there first."

Leaving our bikes in the parking lot, we walked up the path and scanned the front of the building. We searched behind bushes, underneath book drop bins, and around the base of a dry, crumbling fountain. We parted branches, knocked on bricks, and reached as far as we could into book bins. Still, we found nothing.

"What does the app say now?" Dev poked with a stick through moldy leaves that cluttered the fountain.

"The arrow keeps jumping around. Right now it's pointing into the building, toward the back."

"Let's fan out then. You take the right side, I'll take the left, and we'll meet in the rear."

We continued the search, looking for hidden doorways, cellar windows, and weird cracks along the foundation. Meeting by the back door, we checked the app again, only to find it now pointed toward the front.

"When I was on the right side, it was pointing toward the left." I scratched my head.

"Then let's check out the reading on the left side."

Once we reached that side, however, it pointed to the right again.

We trudged back to the front. Dev drew in a sharp breath. "Hey. Do you think whatever we're looking for might be inside the building?"

I looked up from a patch of leafy plants I was sifting through. "Could be, especially since—"

Before I could finish, a car trained its headlights on us.

Dev dived into the fountain, seeking cover in the leaves littering its basin.

I darted behind a bush in the same instant, but the wide beam allowed no escape. Where had the car come from? It must have quietly rolled into the parking lot while we'd searched the back.

Thud! Something dropped into the flower bed. I looked down to see what had made the sound. At that instant, though, a tall figure emerged from the car.

A man's huge frame approached us. A flashlight aimed in our direction.

I lifted my hand to shield my eyes from the light. I peered around the side of the bush but could only make out a silhouette.

It grew larger by the second.

Not daring to breathe, I squatted, transfixed, as the shadowy form advanced.

Not until the man towered over me did I make out his

hat, a police cap. Relief flooded my veins. A cop stood before me, not an armed assailant or a refurbished torso and limbs from *Thirteen Dead Bodies*.

"Good evening, officer." My voice shook as I emerged from the bush.

"You kids don't look like you're returning a library book." The man pulled out a notepad and pen. "Do you mind telling me what exactly you're up to at this hour?"

"We're geocaching, sir." Dev climbed out of the fountain and brushed himself off.

The officer peered at Dev over the top of his glasses. "Pardon me? You're what?"

"Geocaching, sir," Dev said, still swatting at some leaves clinging to his jeans. "We're looking for a cache—a container filled with stuff that's hidden here at the library."

The policeman moistened his lips. "Let me get this straight. You're out here at midnight in the cold, sifting through a moldy fountain, looking for a hidden container?"

"Exactly," I said. "There are actually caches stashed all over the place. Not just here at the library."

"They're in every country of the world." Dev nodded his head eagerly.

"Okay." The man's tone didn't even attempt to conceal his skepticism. "And what do you find in these caches?"

"All kinds of stuff—toys, gear. Sometimes money," Dev explained.

"Treasure hidden all over the world." The officer spoke slowly as he recorded each word. "Just when I thought I'd heard 'em all." He shook his head as he made a few more notes. "Do your parents know you're out here?"

I glanced at Dev but then said, "No, sir. They'd never let us out if we told them our plans."

"Can't imagine why." The policeman circled something with his pen and looked up. "Tell you what, I'm taking your names down but will let you off the hook on the condition that you head straight home. Otherwise I might give your parents a call about this geo-whatever."

"Yes, sir."

We gave him our information. With no choice but to leave, we then took off, each of us heading home.

A loud knocking woke me the next morning. Hearing my mom in the shower, I pulled on some clothes and answered the door. Dev stood on the steps.

"Ready to go?"

"W-What?" I pushed loose curls out of my face.

"Back to the library." Dev let himself in. "We need to check out the inside."

"Oh. Right." I rummaged around for my stuff, digging through the closet and my coat pockets. After a minute I joined Dev on the doorstep.

"Ready?" he asked.

"Yeah, except that we have a problem. I think I lost my phone in a flower bed last night."

* * *

"What?! You lost it?!"

"Yeah," I said. "Let's get over there right away."

At once wide awake, I raced with Dev back to the library. We arrived to find the entrance swarming with patrons. A Brownie troop wearing sashes covered with patches filed, two-by-two, through the main doors. An elderly man advanced in slow motion down the entrance ramp on his walker.

Dev and I lingered at the bike rack, not wanting to arouse suspicion. Finally, the doors stood clear. We scrambled over and searched the flower beds. Before long we found a mud-caked device. It still seemed to work, though. We started the navigation app and hurried through the entrance.

Inside, I shook my head. "Outside, it said the target was thirty feet straight ahead, or somewhere over by the computers." I pointed toward some monitors that stood on tables in the center of the room. "Now that we're in here, I can't get a good reading. Let's just check the entire inside."

"The usual suspects?" Dev asked. "Swiveling bookshelves that hide secret rooms, mist-filled staircases, uneven walls that hint at hidden panels?"

"Don't forget haunted restroom stalls and cleaning closets littered with body parts—"

"Can I help you?"

I looked up. Then my head reeled back. A sleek-looking librarian towered over us. And with her smooth hair, angular features, and wiry frame, she looked a lot like Dragona Mir, the villain Resh Renner had escaped with his hiccup move. She smiled at us, but I could sense her eying my smudged phone maliciously.

I casually lowered it and moved it behind my back. "No, ma'am. We know what we're looking for."

Dragona's insincere smile widened. She looked like she'd rather use a melted chocolate bar as a bookmark than leave us alone in her library, but she turned away.

"Better not get on her bad side," Dev muttered. "She might unleash her army of solar-powered death 'droids on us."

I cringed at the Resh reference, here in this close, public space. "Let's split up."

We wandered through endless rows of shelves piled with countless stacks of books. Soon Dev and I both flapped our lips in frustration. We'd spotted a half-eaten ice cream cone on the tile floor, surrounded by a mucky puddle of melted mint chocolate chip. But aside from it, nothing seemed out of place. And with its open layout, the library looked incapable of harboring anything arcane, let alone a secretive nook.

I motioned Dev over. "Earlier, the arrow pointed toward the computers, but I don't see a way to hide anything there."

"Me neither. Are you sure that thing's still working?"

Dragona glared up at us. She looked like she might spit fire in our direction.

"Yeah," I whispered. "Or at least I think so. It was pointing toward the center of the building last night, too."

"Are the coordinates right? Maybe you misread a four and entered a nine instead or vice versa."

Dev had a good point. I'd once messed up some coordinates, placing a cache in a lake in Canada, instead of a graveyard in New Jersey. Reaching into my pocket, I pulled out the slip of paper that I'd carried around for the past few weeks.

40° 48' 58" N
74° 18' 59" W
Hamilton, Opal B.

"Hamilton, Opal B.," Dev said, looking over my shoulder.

"Everything checks out." I gestured with my phone. "These are the right numbers."

"Hamilton, Opal B.," Dev repeated. "Look, Erin." He pointed to the note. "Why is that name written backwards, with the last name first?"

I stared at the paper. "I don't know." In all the excitement over the coordinates, I had completely forgotten about the words written on it, aside from *Opal*. "That's how you arrange names in alphabetical order, isn't it? Our class lists always come out that way." Years of being seated nearly last, with the name *Schmidt*, had reinforced that fact.

"Card catalogs use the same system, don't they? You always enter the author's last name first when you search for something at the school library."

"The computers!" Finally I caught up with Dev's logic. "All along, we assumed *Opal* was a stone, but maybe it's someone's name. I bet we're supposed to enter that name into the library's search engine!"

We raced over to a free machine. Dragona looked up and bared her teeth.

Dev wagged the mouse back and forth until the display came to life. I then entered "Hamilton, Opal B." into the Search by Author page. After a few seconds, one entry appeared on the screen.

Homestead Days, by Opal B. Hamilton

"There's exactly one book by Opal B. Hamilton!" I jumped up, threw out my arms, and almost squealed along with the Brownie troop members. Their leader had just announced they would earn not one, but two new badges for their library trip. "And it's available." I checked the book's status and made a note of the call number. "It's in the nonfiction section."

Dev and I race-walked to the book's shelf. We skimmed through spine labels but didn't see the book. Even after checking everything again, we still couldn't find anything called *Homestead Days*.

An uneasy feeling filled my insides, as if I had eaten the

melted, spoiled ice cream we'd seen on the floor. "Someone else must know about the book."

"What do you mean?" Dev asked.

"Someone else must have cracked the music box code and found the book." I slumped back against the opposite shelf. Suddenly exhausted from the previous night, I rested my elbow on a volume titled *Beeswax Crafts*.

"And somehow that person checked it out without leaving a trail in the library's system?"

"Exactly. They left no trace of their identity while blocking others from getting hold of it." My foot ran along the spines of the books on the bottom shelf, kicking at a volume with pink ribbons streaming out of its binding. When one of the ribbons caught in my shoe's Velcro fastener, I tried to shake it off but had to lean down to detach it.

The book itself then grabbed my attention. Instead of the usual glossy covering, it was encased in a faded, flowery fabric. Its rough texture tickled my fingers as I grasped its spine and pulled it off the shelf.

Miniature doilies covered the pink fabric on its cover. Scarlet swirls added to its flashiness. I pulled it closer. The scarlet accents looked like letters. In fact, they read, "Homestead Days." I blinked a few times and opened the cover. As if the book somehow sensed my doubt, the title page reiterated, "*Homestead Days*, by Opal B. Hamilton."

I stood transfixed, as if hypnotized by the book's swirling letters. Finally, I found my voice. "Dev? Um... this is the book."

"What?" Dev barely looked up from an ermine skinning guide.

"This is Opal's book, the one we're looking for. It was on the bottom shelf."

Dev dropped the *Dimwits' Complete Handbook of Fur Production* and grabbed *Homestead Days*, staring at the cover. "This is it? This is what all those boxes lead to?" His upper lip curled in disgust. "Is this someone's idea of a joke?" He handed the gaudy volume back to me. "Good luck."

The tacky cover made me want to throw up, too. I'd outgrown flowery textiles in kindergarten, after all.

I shoved it back onto the shelf, hoping no one had spotted me with it. I looked around but then shrank down behind the stacks of books, grabbing Dev and pulling him down at the same time.

"It's Rather Be Fishing!" I whispered. "Harold! The fisherman! He's right over there, talking to Dragona."

"Let's move closer." Dev grabbed my hand. We stepped behind a bookcase near the librarian's desk and crouched down.

"This is the second time this has happened!" Harold did not sound like he'd had a good day fishing. "I've come here to pick up the book, when the system says it's available, yet I can't find it on the shelf."

"What is the book's call number, sir?"

Harold cleared his throat. In a loud, clear voice that indicated he felt all the evil in the world could be blamed on bureaucracy, he rattled off a string of letters and numbers.

"I'm terribly sorry, sir." Dragona clicked and scrolled. "Obviously we track every item in our collection, but occasionally materials do go missing." She shook her head. "I'm afraid it's the only copy in the area, as that title is in high demand." She clicked a few more times. "Our records show the item has been returned. Perhaps it was mis-shelved. Let's take another look in the nonfiction section."

Dev and I exchanged scared looks. They intensified when Harold and Dragona walked across the room toward the aisle with *Homestead Days*.

We followed at a distance on tiptoe and huddled behind a puppet theater in the children's area.

"It should be here on this shelf." Dragona pointed to the shelf with Opal's book.

My breathing grew shallow. If only I'd held onto the book, Harold wouldn't have had a chance at it. If only I'd borrowed a phone last week, I might have come here days ago. I gripped the edges of the puppet theater, practically crushing its cardboard frame.

"I told you," Harold said. "I've already looked there."

"You are absolutely right, sir." Dragona scanned the shelves. "I cannot locate that title at this time. What I can do, however, is put it on reserve for you. The library staff will notify you as soon as it turns up and will hold it at the circulation desk until you pick it up."

"That's nice of you, but I need it now." Harold shook his head. "Don't bother. It'll be too late." He spun on his heel and stomped toward the exit.

"That was close," I said as Dev and I crawled out from behind the theater.

"Do you think he was looking for the same book?"

"I'm sure of it." I raced back over to the aisle, not caring how many scowls I elicited from Dragona. Glitzy or not, I had to check out the book. I grabbed it off the shelf and made a beeline for the circulation desk.

My foot tapped the floor as I stood in line. The librarian behind the desk seemed oblivious to my impatience and to the number of people waiting. Besides checking out books, she also verified each item's data in the system and highlighted due dates on printouts. In addition, she reminded each patron of the new fee table. Then, in case these efforts to hold up traffic failed, she chatted with everyone who approached the desk, pausing between bleeps of the scanner to dish out the latest gossip or to exclaim, "No!" and clap her hands whenever someone shared a particularly scandalous story.

I hugged the book to my chest, afraid someone would steal it from me. Three people still stood ahead of me in line. None of them could have reserved it, right?

When the woman in front of me turned and gave me a once-over, I managed to stop my foot from tapping. I also took a deep breath and relaxed my grip on the book.

My terror returned, however, when Pierce, the hulk-bodied chess team captain, suddenly snagged the book out of my hands.

"What's this?" Pierce taunted in a deep, hoarse voice. "A romance? How sweet! Trying to impress your boyfriend?" His eyes flitted to Dev as he flaunted the book and then held it high up over my head.

I felt my face grow as scarlet as the cover's lettering. "Give it back."

Pierce beamed. "You admit it? You seriously want to check this out? Got a bad crush?" Again, he glanced at Dev before lowering the book and giving it another wave.

I refused to take the bait. But Dev had heard every word. Now he'd think I'd told people we were going out. My cheeks grew so hot, I thought I would melt on the spot into a mucky puddle like the abandoned ice cream. The Brownies would earn yet another badge by cleaning up the mess.

Pierce waved the book again. I could just tell him, "Not mine. I found it on the floor and thought it needed to be re-shelved." Assuming no one else got to it first, I'd come back later and check it out, preferably without an audience.

But if someone beat me to it, it might be months before I got hold of it. Some people renewed items over and over or returned them late or lost them. Week after week, I would lie awake at night, wondering what secrets the book held.

No matter the price, I couldn't face that scenario.

Pierce lowered the book and then whisked it up high. But before he could say anything, Dragona materialized out of the blue, confirming Dev's suspicions that she possessed atom-swapping powers. "This is library property, Pierce." She plucked the book from his hands. "And you are twelve minutes late for your community service appointment. I suggest you hustle back to Mrs. Iron's office, where she is waiting for you." When Pierce made no sign of moving, she added, "I assure you, the longer you keep her, the more creative she will be in finding pleasant tasks for you to accomplish." She emphasized the word *pleasant* in a way that made it sound far from fun. Turning to me, she asked, "Does this belong to you, young lady?"

I felt the weight of the other patrons' stares. It took everything in me, but somehow I managed to mutter, "Yes, ma'am." Then I checked out the book.

Chapter 9

All the way home, I wondered about the book. What mysteries would it reveal? Too embarrassed to let anyone see it, I waited until locked in my room before opening its chintzy cover. Holding it at arm's length, I flipped through it, turning each page with the very tips of two fingers, as if I were handling a snotty tissue Marcus had left on the bathroom floor. Opal had handwritten it in diary format, using an old-fashioned cursive font that made it hard to get through. It didn't help that its story wasn't exactly gripping.

I sighed and tossed it onto my bed. My lips let out a moan when a small cloud of dust rose up around it.

As the dirt settled on my covers, my head dropped to my chest. If only Dad were here, he'd help me through the diary. He would find it fascinating because of its archaeological value. He would point out historically significant passages and help me decipher the odd writing style. Without his help, though, getting to the bottom of each page would feel like doing community service in the library.

I fumbled around for my phone and opened a chat window.

Erin: Uncle El?

I picked up a pen and doodled for a minute.

Erin: We figured out the wooden boxes, but all we have is a dusty diary.

Frowning, I continued.

Erin: I almost died getting it. Pierce teased me about its flowery cover in front of the entire library. What kind of school is this where the chess captains are bullies?

I'd sacrificed my social status at the checkout desk, yet the diary had gotten me nowhere. A shudder ran up my spine. Undoubtedly Pierce would have a lot of fun with the romance theme the next few times I ran into him. He'd make a point of bringing it up in front of Dev again.

The paper I'd doodled on now had holes in it. I brushed aside the shreds and turned back to my phone.

Erin: Am I crazy to read the diary?

My fingers ran over the tattered book's smooth pages. Years of wear had left all but one of its four corners dog-eared and rounded.

Erin: Dev thinks it's a joke.

Uncle El: How about a break? Some music for you...

Emojis danced across my screen, and my e-mail beeped as an audio file of saxophone music arrived. The name of the piece looked familiar. Had Uncle El sent it before? I scratched my head. Uh, oh. He had, the last time we'd texted. And I'd never listened to it. In fact, I'd hung up on him.

Oops. I felt like hiding under the homework papers and heaps of dirty laundry scattered across my floor. When the emojis started tap-dancing and giggling, though, I hit *Play*.

The cool, haunting tones of the alto sax washed over me. By the time it came to an end, I'd stopped shredding papers with my pen.

The song had reminded me I hadn't practiced for days, so I put my horn together and went through my pieces. The music boxes came to mind. Maybe if I combined their melodies, the three would form a song, just like the numbers in their messages formed coordinates.

Macaw's message had the degrees, so its notes came first. Next came Magpie's, since it held the second part of the coordinates. I finished up with Quail's melody.

Strangely, when I reached the end, I felt like a conductor had cut me off, mid-measure, abruptly stopping the show. The tune didn't resolve nicely, the way most pieces did at their close. It seemed incomplete.

I sat up straight. A missing line meant there was something left to find, like another box.

The diary still rested on my covers. Maybe it would unlock the secret of the boxes' message. With its single pointy corner and jigsaw designs, it reminded me of a corner piece in a puzzle, one that helps make sense out of everything by linking different parts together into a clear picture.

Erin: Over & out.

I put away my sax and opened the shabby book. Maybe its tattered pages would lead to another box. I just hoped it contained something other than bird feathers.

* * *

"Please turn to page fifty-two of your text, where you'll find a time line detailing Jacques Cartier's pursuit of riches. Using that information, complete the worksheet on your tablets." Mrs. Dearg's voice rang through the history room on Monday morning.

As I worked on the second question, a window popped up on my screen.

How's the romance going?

I coughed to cover up a chuckle. Dev had sent the instant message. When Mrs. Dearg turned her back, I tapped a reply.

Love birds, nesting robins, feather pillows.

The previous night, I'd finished a diary entry about collecting goose down to use in bedding.

I searched for the *Send* button but got distracted. Pierce sat nearby, peering around another student to read the words on my tablet.

I leaned over to block his view. How much had he seen? Worse, what would he do with the information? If he called Dev my boyfriend again, my cheeks would spontaneously combust, and Dev would hitch a ride on the next Resh-mobile to another galaxy.

Click! Before I could toggle back to the worksheet, Mrs. Dearg whisked past me and snapped a picture of my screen with her phone. Continuing on to the front of the room, she scanned the captured image. She then faced the class and cleared her throat.

My stomach lurched. Forget about Pierce. Mrs. Dearg was about to inflict more serious damage. The entire school would soon associate me with romances, feather pillows, and love birds.

After a long moment, Mrs. Dearg announced, "No homework today." Whoops and hurrahs erupted from the class. "I didn't have time to prepare anything," she explained. "I got back late last night from a marching band competition, where my husband's drum corps took first prize, and my flute choir placed an honorable third." After the cheers died down, she narrowed her eyes. "Erin and Deval, I'd like to speak to you after class."

I slumped in my seat, relieved she hadn't read my words out loud. But when I turned back to the worksheet, I had about as much success as Cartier on his fruitless quest for gold.

After class, Dev and I slunk over to Mrs. Dearg's desk.

"Well, well," she began. "Congratulations that your romance has progressed to the stage where" — she glanced at the image, still on her phone — "where you are ready to settle down like a flock of birds." Sliding her glasses down to a bump on the tip of her knobbly nose, she looked directly at Dev and then at me. "My apologies, also. Cartier's exploits must seem a tedious trifle when compared with feather pillows."

I stared at my feet.

"Or have I misinterpreted this message?" she asked.

"Yes, Mrs. Dearg." Dev looked up and smiled. In fact, he almost laughed.

In contrast, I almost wet my pants.

"You're both good kids with bright futures." Mrs. Dearg dabbed her gnarled nose with a tissue. "I'm thrilled to have you in my class. But don't start down the wrong path. I understand that most students' personal lives are far more interesting than Cartier's travels. However, for the fifty minutes I see you each day, I need you to focus on the subject at hand."

"Got it, Mrs. Dearg," Dev said. I nodded.

"To ensure you understand that school computers are not to be used for personal communication, I suggest you complete an additional review sheet on Cartier, plus an essay on Melbourne's role in the Victorian Gold Rush."

"What!?" Dev asked.

I teetered, as if on Cartier's ship during a storm.

"Or should I call the main office and have Principal Candus read your love notes over the daily announcements?"

"We will gladly do the extra work, Mrs. Dearg," Dev answered.

I nodded my agreement, probably looking like one of

Marcus's Resh bobble-heads.

* * *

"What's the deal with the love birds?" Dev asked on our way to the ballpark after school.

I risked a glance at him, shocked he'd bring up the subject again. He didn't seem squirmy about it, though. "The book is a diary," I answered quickly, glad to change the subject. "Some girl named Opal Hamilton wrote it in the early 1900s. It tells all about farm life one hundred years ago."

"So what's the connection to the boxes?" Dev peered into a fountain at the park entrance. Before hitting a few balls, he hoped to find a new cache someone had hidden in the basin.

"So far, just the birds. They're all over the diary. One day it talks about a robin making a nest on the farm. Another day it says something about blue jays squawking at barn cats."

"Sounds like the family was infatuated with them." Dev leaned over the fountain and scanned the rim.

"Yeah. Plus, it was The Bird Watchers who launched the wooden boxes."

Dev crossed to the other side of the fountain and reached straight into some slimy green algae to detach a small container.

I clutched my stomach. I must have gotten Dev addicted to geocaching. We'd once seen the name Chain Cacher in a log. Was he now as hooked as a chain-smoker is to cigarettes?

"I'm not convinced we're on the right track." Dev opened the cache's lid and pulled out a soggy logbook.

"Me neither." I edged back as Dev wiped green goop on his jeans.

"Can't we just e-mail The Bird Watchers?" Dev returned

the cache. "Or are you enjoying the details of Opal's personal life?"

"Yeah, those stories of love birds building nests in the chicken coop are right up my alley." I smiled and tried to sound casual, but the whole romance topic still made me edgy. I tossed Dev a ball. Something else bothered me, too. I already had e-mailed The Bird Watchers, right after I'd found the first box. But they'd never replied.

That evening, I pulled out my phone.

Erin: Uncle El? I need to talk again.

I picked at a ragged hangnail for a long moment.

Erin: About Dev.

The blood didn't rush to my head. It stampeded, nearly drowning my nose as it reddened my cheeks.

Erin: Pierce called Dev my boyfriend at the library. And he saw my message to Dev about the diary. Then Mrs. Dearg talked about our "romance."

I knit my brow. Pierce had also approached our table at lunch. The jicama-burger casserole I'd downed had sprouted writhing worms as I'd pictured him whipping out a megaphone and informing the lunchroom of my engagement to Dev. In the end, he'd only banged into our table, sending whole-grains flying, but visions of him haunted me. Most involved e-mails filled with heart emojis going viral.

Erin: Dev's really popular, too. So if rumors

start, everyone will believe them. Who wouldn't want to go out with Dev?

I looked back down at my hangnail as I thought of all the girls at school who followed Dev around and never missed a chance to shoot glares in my direction.

My phone buzzed.

Uncle El: Ahem.

Had someone cleared their throat? I shook my head. I must have imagined it, but suddenly I felt more at ease than a kid in grandma's lap. No matter what I said, Uncle El could take it.

Erin: I like hanging out with Dev, but what if people start saying things about us? Will it drive Dev away?

A moan escaped my throat. It sounded like the groan of a bus's engine as it pulled away from the stop outside my window.

My in-box flashed. Uncle El had forwarded me an e-mail, part of an ongoing conversation between me and Dev.

I skimmed through it, not caring how Uncle El had gotten hold of it. He undoubtedly had ties to intelligence agencies. But why had he sent it? I took a closer look.

Dev: The new Resh watch goes on sale this weekend. Want to come to the mall with me to get it? The shop might also have some discounted Dragona geo trackers.

Erin: Should we also get you a Resh costume, complete with a cape, to make your geekdom official?

I got up and paced around my room.

Erin: Dev's fun, isn't he?

I paced some more.

Erin: It's never hard to talk to Dev.

I sat down on the edge of my bed. Dev had actually smiled when Mrs. Dearg had read the love notes out loud. He hadn't looked at all embarrassed.

Erin: Dev's a really good friend.

I'd once had a crush on Nate, a boy who moved away after fifth grade. Seeing him had made me as jittery as Monday morning of exam week. With Dev, though, it always felt like the weekend.

I exhaled. I didn't have all the answers. But then again, who did?

Erin: Over & out.

Chapter 10

I read as much as I could in the diary over the next few days. Its long-winded, sleep-inducing style and curlicue font didn't make it easy, though.

Most afternoons I pushed the book aside after a few pages and took a break to look for yard work. I'd looked for work over the summer without any luck, after Mom cut my allowance. But now that autumn leaves had started to fall, there was money to be made cleaning them up.

"Steve Fogarta takes care of most lawns on this street," one woman told me, after I'd knocked on her door. She pointed to a man unloading equipment from a white van. When he looked up and waved, she waved back. "He pretty much has a monopoly on the area, even though his prices are steep. But he's reliable and friendly."

Before heading back, I tried a few more doors but got the same story.

Homework also kept me from making progress in the diary. I checked my assignment pad one night, sure I'd completed everything and could finally delve back into Opal's entries on dressing hens and plucking goose feathers. One unfinished task glared back at me, though: current events. I groaned and dropped my head onto my desk.

When I finally managed to look up again, I dug a newspaper out of the recycling bin but could only find articles about trout sushi: maps showing fishing hot spots, marinades stolen from a rare copy of *Guarded Recipes*, and skinning guides. They'd devoted the entire issue to the fad. I gripped the edge of my chair as my gaze fell on a graphic image demonstrating proper cleaning technique.

Giving up on the assignment, I tossed the newspaper aside and headed upstairs to make some headway in the diary. Maybe I'd find the missing strain of the wooden boxes' song tucked into the back or a symphony score whose notes functioned as clues. I just hoped they led to something other than a bird sanctuary.

"Secret chambers?" Dev asked me after school the next day as we headed down to the buses.

"Yeah. The diary said the Hamiltons expanded their ice cellar. They added an underground storage area to it."

"On their farm?" Dev hopped up on the railing and slid down toward the exit.

"Exactly." I rolled my eyes when several girls broke into applause over Dev's stunt. "There were break-ins at some of their neighbors. The Hamiltons had a big discussion about how to keep their stuff safe. They ended up digging a tunnel leading to hidden rooms."

"A tunnel?"

"Yeah. It started in the ice cellar and led to a storage room. But somewhere off the tunnel was a secret opening."

"Cool." Dev turned red and hurried outside as the girls held the door open for him. They tried to let it slam in my face, but Dev caught it and ushered me through. "Where did it go?"

"It led to another area, where they stored valuables."

"Valuables? What kind of valuables? I thought they were poor farmers."

"That's what I thought. The diary only talks about money they earned from crops, eggs, and livestock."

"Weird." Dev looked around and blew air from his cheeks when the girls headed a different way. "I mean, the tunnel network's really fascinating, but it seems like an awful lot of trouble just to hide some cash."

"You're right," I admitted. "And not only that, but the family kept a few basic things like canned food and candles near the tunnel entrance to fool burglars. Anyone entering the tunnel would spot the supplies and think they'd found everything, not realizing that the more valuable stuff was hidden deeper."

"Clever." Dev donned his Resh Renner sunglasses and held his bag up to hide his face as another group of girls approached us, giggling and whispering. "But what were they hiding?"

"The diary doesn't say, except that it was a lot of trouble to move everything later. When Opal was much older, they sold the farm and moved into a house here in Northlawn. The new house had a bomb shelter, which they expanded to use as storage space."

"A bomb shelter? What for? Did burglars carry ballistic missiles back then?"

"Not sure." I turned to board my bus. "I only know World War Two was going on at the time, and all the houses in the neighborhood had shelters with interconnecting tunnels."

"Hmm. Sounds like they had a small fortune in there, or whatever they valued—maybe their collection of bird carcasses in jars of formaldehyde."

* * *

I nearly boiled over with excitement later that night as I finished the diary. I started to call Dev but then stopped, blinking in disbelief. My clock read 11:28.

By the time I got to school the next day, steam practically puffed out of my ears. "I got to the end of the diary," I burst out as soon as Dev entered the science room. He'd asked me to meet him there before school. "And you'll never guess what was tucked away in the back."

"A treasure map? Another set of coordinates? A pop-up diagram showing a rare bird's anatomy?"

"No." I waved away his comments. "A sheet of music."

Dev stared at me blankly as he filled a watering can.

"Music notes," I explained. "But most of the page was torn out. The first line was still there, though. It was the song the wooden boxes play."

"Oh." Dev's face lit up. He looked like Resh had become real and enlisted him as an accomplice. "Hey, weren't you going to e-mail The Bird Watchers earlier this week?"

"I did, but they haven't gotten back to me." Just like the first time, they hadn't responded.

Dev watered several dirt-filled cups labeled with his name.

"What are we actually doing here?" I poked at the soil in one of the cups.

"My seeds aren't growing."

"I can see that." I poured out some murky water that had collected in the base of a cup. "When do you need the results?"

"By Monday." Dev gave each cup a few more drops, including the one I'd just drained. "I thought some extra care might help them sprout. Maybe some music, too." He looked around. Seeing no one, he sneaked out his phone. "I bet plants like country." The twang of a steel guitar filled the room as Dev hit *Play*. He lifted a cup and twirled around with it while humming along to a tune about whiskey and gravel roads.

I opened my mouth to comment on his choice of music but then held my tongue. At least he hadn't started the Resh soundtrack.

"You know, this mystery reminds me of the Steaming Cauldron cache." Dev set down the plant and adjusted a blind to let in more light. "We only had limited information then, but once we put it all together, we were able to work it out."

"You're right. This whole thing is kind of convoluted." I tried not to stare at Pierce, who stood outside the window near the recycling and garbage bins, pretending to use one as a urinal as students filed past him into the school. "We never get the information directly. Instead we have to decrypt clues from pieces of coordinates and a diary with missing pages."

"Yeah." Dev gave one of the cups an encouraging pat.

"Maybe if we use the same strategy now, we'll figure out the next step."

Dev raised his eyebrows. "Could be worth it. The wooden boxes did hint at riches with their ancient-looking treasure maps."

"And the diary talks about secret chambers where valuables were stored."

"Right." Dev turned down the volume, leaned in, and dropped his voice to a whisper. "The Hamiltons must have been hiding more than just a huge wad of cash."

"They did go to a lot of effort to protect their prized possessions." I picked at some dirt under my fingernail. "You don't think they stowed away some kind of fortune somewhere, do you?"

Dev shrugged and then turned the volume back up. "Either that or a collection of out-of-print field guides to New World birds."

His comment barely registered with me. The idea of fortune had triggered a flood of images. I pictured Dad coming home. Forget about plane tickets to Hawaii. He'd return for good if we had a pile of riches. It would solve all our money problems. We'd spend weekends geocaching again, instead of catching up on the laundry. We could build a new hideout. Our old yard had one in a shack, with reclining airplane seats and a lava lamp. Maybe we'd adopt a dog, too, something we'd once talked about.

Dev lifted a cup up high and serenaded it as the chorus swelled. When a guitar solo cut in, he set it back down. "So... where'd they hide it?"

"Well..." I tilted my head to the side. "The Bird Watchers launched three boxes from the woods: one going east, one south, and the third west. Together, they point to the diary, through their hidden coordinates."

"What does the diary point to?"

"It doesn't mention any locations besides the farm and a house in Northlawn."

"And where was the farm located?"

"The diary never says." I narrowed my eyes. "In fact, it doesn't even give a state."

Dev square-danced around with another plant, sending clumps of soil flying. "So the treasure is likely in Northlawn."

I brushed dirt off my sleeve. "Why Northlawn?"

"Because it lies north of the woods." Dev pounded the lab table with his fist, scattering more dirt.

"Right, but what does that have to do with anything?" I leaned back to escape future soil assaults.

"It makes perfect sense to me." Dev gestured wildly. "If someone hid treasure somewhere, they wouldn't just spoon feed the location to everyone. They'd make it difficult to find. They'd send the clues in completely different directions—like east, south, and west—all moving away from the booty in the north."

"Interesting." I grabbed the end cup before Dev could knock it over. "Supposing you're right, the treasure must be hidden in the house in Northlawn that the Hamilton family bought in 1945."

"Exactly, assuming the house still exists."

I shot him a questioning look.

"It might have been torn down by now," Dev elaborated. "For all we know, the township might have converted the property into green space or a retail zone. A big box chain might occupy that address or even a bean field." He gestured with one of the cups as the bell rang.

* * *

"Do you think anyone else is onto this?" Dev asked later that afternoon as I let him into my apartment. Over black bean pate at lunch, we'd decided to research the Hamilton's Northlawn address on the Internet.

"Rather Be Fishing and Fife & Drum are definitely still threats." I pulled the table showing the boxes' locations out of my pocket.

Dev looked up from examining Marcus's Resh Renner invisible ink pen. "Have they both seen Magpie?" He took the table from me.

"Rather Be Fishing visited Steaming Cauldron but didn't take Magpie." I pointed to Rather Be Fishing's row on my table. "Who knows? Maybe he didn't even see it."

Dev rolled his eyes back far enough to overextend an optic muscle.

	Quail	Magpie	Macaw
Fife-And-Drum	Moved it out of the woods.	Picked it up from Steaming-Cauldron.	Moved it from History-Geeks-Delight to Karaoke-Candy.
Rather-Be-Fishing	Had it and moved it west on fishing trip.	Visited Steaming-Cauldron when Magpie was in it, but didn't take it.	Moved it out of the woods.
Water-Break (me)	Saw it in Rather-Be-Fishing's shed.	Moved it from woods to Steaming-Cauldron.	Saw it in Karaoke-Candy.

I held up my hands in defense. "I haven't gone all soft. I've been watching Harold's logs, and he hasn't had any trackables for weeks." We went into the living room. I kicked aside a *Gadgets Galore* magazine that Marcus had left on the floor. "But his cache count is way up."

"And what about Fife & Drum?" Dev picked up the magazine.

"She took Magpie from Steaming Cauldron." I pointed to Fife & Drum on my table. "That worries me, but I don't think she's seen the diary. I've had it since last Thursday, and I doubt anyone checked it out before me."

"How do you know?"

"They wouldn't have returned it. It's only been a month since the wooden boxes were launched. Anyone who had it could have kept it until now without even paying an overdue fine."

Remembering our mission of finding the Hamiltons' address, I opened a browser. The County Clerk's web page reported some bad news, though. The county had an impressive collection of all documents associated with property transactions for the past few centuries. But it was paper. In other words, we'd have to go through the Record Room files manually.

I slumped in my seat.

Dev sat up straighter, though, and actually dropped the magazine. "Cool!"

I cringed at his cheery tone. He sounded like a cheerleader who'd just downed a gallon-sized energy drink.

"The Record Room—I can see it already." His voice had turned dreamy. "A dark, windowless room in the basement with wilted plants and a ceiling filled with ductwork."

"It probably also has lots of dilapidated microfiche readers, complete with burned-out light bulbs and stubborn, loud-clicking power switches." I jabbed a pen into a pad of paper.

"Definitely." Dev rubbed his palms together. "File cabinets line the long, narrow aisles, along with towers of teetering shelves stuffed with documents."

I picked up a Resh Renner action figure and hit Dev over the head with it.

"And dusty, clunky monitors sit in cobweby corners, humming loudly. A gum-snapping secretary greets us with an annoyed look when we arrive. Her voice sounds like loose microfiche screws scratching a blackboard. A ghost who haunts the stacks hovers above us as we search. This could be loads of fun!"

I brandished the Resh figure again. I also scrolled down on the county web site.

"Wait a second." I leaned in to read the fine print. "Online queries are also available!"

"What?" Dev shook his head.

"Yeah, let's give it a whirl." I entered Opal's name and the year 1945. I held my breath as I pressed *Go*.

Progress dots appeared and spun in a circle. Elevator music started playing. We waited for a minute or so, my foot tapping the entire time. The dots kept circling but slowed down. Then the page went dim. Just when I expected smoke to rise from the speakers, the site finally churned out some gobbledygook.

Dev and I both scooted up to the computer.

"What does that mean?" he asked.

"Not sure. It kind of looks like a cartoon character swearing."

He tilted his head sideways. "I think this is an address." He pointed to the screen. "I think it says '275 Hidden Path Drive.'"

"Yeah. It looks like Opal purchased some property at 275 Hidden Path Drive in 1945."

"So we've got it!" Dev bumped my knuckles and hiccupped loudly in a salute to Resh Renner.

"Well," I added. "Assuming there's still a Hidden Path Drive in Northlawn."

* * *

We pored over a map of Northlawn right away.

"Yes!" Dev jumped up and struck a superhero pose.

I merely smiled. Hidden Path Drive still existed. I felt more relieved than when I'd realized the recall on Resh Renner shampoo, due to reports of hair loss, did not apply to the variety Marcus had stocked in our bathroom.

Dev had to watch his sister again that evening, but the next day, we set out on our bikes to find the property or whatever was left of it. After riding through town, we turned onto Hidden Path Drive. At last, after rounding numerous bends, we reached Two Seventy-Five. A house stood on the lot. We pulled over to get a closer look.

I scratched my head. Maybe I'd pictured a sinister manor, shaded and obscured by thick, overgrown hedges that gave it an abandoned look, as if it harbored a dark, long-forgotten mystery. Or possibly a regal-looking fortress had come to mind, with defenses strong enough to guard a mound of riches.

The house that stood before us, however, looked ordinary. In fact, I couldn't imagine anything less likely to safeguard a secret. Covered in sunny yellow siding and trimmed with bright white shutters, it had a tidy, cheery look and projected an innocent, fairytale-like aura.

"Wait a second." I rapped my nails on my handlebars.

"I've been to this house before."

"Really?" Dev lost his grip on his bike. He lurched to catch it before it crashed to the ground.

"Yeah." I stared at the house. "I think my mom knows the people who live here, sort of."

"What do you mean?"

"I'm pretty sure we brought them a meal once."

"Hmm." Dev's eyebrows shot up, and his nostrils flared. "Feel like ringing the doorbell?"

I turned to Dev. "What? And say I've come to claim the treasure?"

"Good point." Dev circled around on his bike.

It seemed silly that we'd worried about the house existing because now we faced a bigger problem. With a little planning, searching an abandoned building or an empty lot would have been easier than finding a geocache with a difficulty level of two or three. Uncovering something inside a well-maintained house, on the other hand, could pose a few problems, if not impossibilities. We might as well try to reach the cache on the International Space Station.

"Nice tree." Dev pointed at a tall maple in the front yard. "A good place for a geocache."

I looked up. Filled with hollows and crooks, the tree's thick trunk did have at least ten ideal spots for small containers.

"We could ask if we can hide a cache in their tree."

I shook my head. "Let's move on before someone sees us." We continued down the street.

"Did you notice the For Sale sign?" Dev shouted as we turned the corner. "We could pretend we're interested in buying it and ask to look around."

"We're too young to be taken seriously."

"Then maybe your mom could make them some food,

and we could offer to deliver it."

"My mom doesn't have time to cook anymore, and we only brought them something because they'd had surgery. I don't think we can just show up now with a casserole."

A white van swerved around us. "Maybe we could come back at night," I said. "We could snoop around the outside for a cellar door."

"That style of house doesn't have an outside cellar." Dev shook his head. "My cousins used to live in one just like it on the other side of town. But we could spy on the house. We might catch somebody hiding a key in a flowerpot or under a mat."

"And then what?"

"We could sneak in when nobody's home." Dev raised his eyebrows again.

"No, thanks." Memories of Harold's shed still gave me bad dreams. "In fact, maybe there's no point in pursuing the whole thing. Even if we manage to get inside and find something valuable, it would belong to the owners."

Dev opened his mouth to comment, but no words came out, even though I'd never seen him fail to think his way out of a pickle.

The wind picked up as we pedaled side by side. I stayed next to Dev, blocking half the road as the howling of a strong gust filled my ears. Suddenly a horn blared, making us both jump. A red pickup then drove past. It gunned its engine while it swerved around Dev and me.

"He nearly hit us!" Dev shook his hands at the truck.

"He didn't even give us a chance to move aside. I would have pulled back if I'd known he was there."

"Hey, look! It's Rather Be Fishing! See the back of the truck?"

I followed Dev's gaze. Just before the pickup sped out of view, I caught a glimpse of the iridescent sticker on its rear with its splashing waves and fish.

My pulse quickened. Did Harold sense we'd spent an evening in his shed? He was probably plotting torturous revenge. He also might have seen us near the house on Hidden Path Drive.

Chapter 11

"I've got to head home," Dev said once we'd reached the end of the street. "My great-aunt's birthday party is this afternoon." He went on to grumble about family events overflowing with nosy, nagging relatives who told corny jokes and tried to map out his future.

I listened but couldn't really sympathize. The attention didn't sound all that bad to me. And neither did the festive food and music. At least his family was still together.

In contrast, I faced an afternoon alone. Mom had e-mailed me a list of chores to tackle while Marcus spent the afternoon at a robotics fair and she finished up a project at work.

Following Mom's instructions, I started the washer and dryer. Next I pulled out my phone and opened a text window. Not sure how to begin, I wandered around the apartment. Finally I settled down on a step stool in the laundry room.

Gazing through the glass door of the dryer, I watched the clothes tumbling for a while.

Erin: Uncle El? Are you there?

Uncle El: You okay?

Erin: What to do now?

When Uncle El didn't answer right away, I dropped my head, studying the clothes again. Finally, I elaborated.

Erin: I just wanted to help my family. If I found valuables, maybe we'd get our hideout back.

Even with its wobbly steps and faint, mildewy smell, the hideout had still made a great getaway for Marcus and me and our friends. Neighborhood pets had also loved it, and Dad had once talked about getting a dog.

Erin: Maybe Dad could come home, too.

I turned away, thinking of the last time I'd talked to my father. He'd mentioned extending his stay in Hawaii to earn more money.

Erin: Now even if Dev & I find something at the house, it would belong to someone else.

I crossed my arms over my chest.

Erin: And if we don't find anything, we'll never figure out where the music box clues lead or why someone launched them.

The dryer kept spinning. I frowned. No matter which angle I viewed everything from, I saw no hope. Like the clothes tumbling around and around, my family seemed caught in an endless cycle of misery. Even if Dad earned some money in Hawaii, we would start spending it as soon as he got home. Then he'd have to look for more work. And most likely he'd end up in another remote corner of the world, landing us in the same situation.

I sat on the stool for a while. Finally the dryer beeped, signaling the end of the cycle. In the same instant, my e-mail chimed as a new message arrived.

Uncle El had sent the mail. It contained a trailer from an old Resh Renner movie.

I wilted. What did Resh have to do with anything? Worse, it looked like Uncle El still liked him, too. He'd probably also joined the fan club. Or maybe one of his Hollywood sources had sent the link. He had lots of friends in high places.

I blinked a few times, trying not to picture Uncle El at a Resh convention, in costume. Then I hit *Play*, holding the phone as far away as possible, as if it had fallen into a pile of Marcus's dirty underwear.

The clip showed Resh stranded on a deserted planet, using magnetic rocks to repair his hover-mobile. I shook my head. Crippled aircraft said nothing to me. I reloaded the dryer and trudged up the stairs with the clean laundry.

At the top, I remembered Marcus watching that movie when Dad was leaving for Hawaii. I only thought of it because Mom had cited that very scene right after Dad left. "Just like Resh Renner using magnetite to repair his hover-mobile," she'd told Marcus, "we'll have to manage the best with what we have."

I set the laundry down. Mom could be really geeky sometimes. *Manage the best with what we have?* I had nothing at the moment besides lots of chores to do.

I folded some shirts and could only see myself mired

in gloom. The house at 275 Hidden Path Drive loomed over me like an impenetrable fortress. I was locked outside, probably floundering in its mucky moat. I even pictured Dev beside me in the murky water.

A smile twitched at my lips. Most likely Dev was sculpting with the mud or devising a scheme to haul it home by the cartload, so his mother and sisters could enjoy a rejuvenating bath. My smile widened as I thought back on Dev and some of his sillier schemes, like fishing a geocache out of slimy green algae, distracting Ms. Mode with the trout sushi craze, and square-dancing to country with his bean seeds. Maybe I did have something—Dev, although having him as a friend didn't solve my family's problems. But it certainly made things more fun.

What else had I overlooked? I folded some more laundry, but sifting through clothes and searching for missing socks only made me think of all the obstacles I'd faced: the cryptic clues we couldn't understand; the wasps targeting us in the woods; the policeman questioning us at the library; the chintzy diary no one wanted to check out.

I sat down. Maybe I had something there, too. Through it all, I'd never given up. I'd survived Pierce's taunts and an evening locked in Rather Be Fishing's shed, after all. Maybe simply sticking with our mission counted for something, too.

I pushed the laundry aside. My hand brushed against Marcus's underwear, but I didn't care. I just dialed Dev's number.

He answered right away amid loud music and yelps from either his little sister or dog. I had trouble telling the two apart. "I think we should keep at it," I said. "We've come so far, and we know from the diary that the house is hiding some secret."

"Absolutely. We might not have all the answers, but we can't give up now."

"And even if we only figure out where the clues lead, it'd still be worth it to solve this mystery."

"Let's go for it!" Dev had to shout as some drumbeats in the background intensified. "Anything to get me away from these nagging relatives. Plus, we might dig up something huge! And if the owners don't want to share the fortune, they still might reward us for finding it."

"True." It didn't make sense that Dev wanted to find the treasure to escape his family while I needed it to reunite mine. But I smiled anyway, glad to have Dev on board.

* * *

Over the next few days I kept looking for yard work. Until we got our reward, I needed the cash. No one agreed to hire me on the spot, but I did make a list of potential addresses.

Dev and I also brainstormed about searching the Hamilton residence.

"We could pose as meter readers," he suggested at the school's Halloween dance as a stray piece of cheesecloth fell in his face. His mummy costume was starting to unwind.

"We'd have to disguise our age," I yelled back as everyone fled the dance floor. A slow song had just started up.

Dev grasped my shoulder to stop me and leaned in. My heart skipped a beat when, for a second, I thought he might ask me to dance. "The Slime Busters," he yelled instead over the loud music. "We could work as a waterproofing team: The Slime Busters."

I looked up at him and raised my hands in a helpless gesture.

"That house is near Mystery Hills Lake." His head wrap unraveled further. "The owners are bound to have had water damage at some point. We'd have at least a half an hour in the place, pretending to remove mold."

I shook my head and steered him toward the punch bowl.

Finally, on the way to the buses one day the next week, I feared I'd befriended a lunatic. "We could tell the people at 275 Hidden Path Drive we're from the future," Dev said. He'd stopped, mid-stride in a packed hallway. "Seriously," he protested as Ms. Mode tried to herd people past him, cringing every time a student brushed against her handstitched Parisian shoulder bag. "I could claim to have seen my mother falling in love with the house, then my family buying it, and finally, my baby sister tumbling down the stairs to her death, all in the future."

"Not sure I follow you." I steered clear of the now fuming Ms. Mode.

"And now I've traveled back in time to prevent the tragedy."

"How?"

"By talking the owners into changing the paint so my mom won't like it and won't buy it. We'd have an excuse to go through the entire place."

I smiled but shook my head. "There must be another way."

Mom was sitting at the kitchen table when I got back from school. She peered up from her screen as I came in. "I had a dentist's appointment this afternoon, so I've been working from home since then," she explained.

I poured myself a glass of milk.

"Hey, I was in your room, putting away some laundry," she said. "I noticed a paper with addresses on your desk. Are those your potential clients?"

"Yeah." I sat down with her. "I've been scouting out a few neighborhoods, looking for yard work. But no bites yet."

"That's sad." Mom drained her coffee.

"Tell me about it." It was bad enough that Dad had lost his job. Now I couldn't find work either. I helped myself to another glass of milk, thrilled not to be drinking the hemp milk the school now served.

"Can I have some of that?" Mom took the jug from me and fixed herself another cup of coffee. She was actually drinking from a mug. Our funds must have dropped pretty low. She used to take cream in her coffee, not milk. And she'd buy it at the corner cafe instead of brewing it herself.

I slumped down in a chair. People might start bringing us meals, just like we used to cook for others in need. Then I sat up straight, struck by an idea. "Mom. Doesn't someone from our congregation live on Hidden Path Drive? We brought them a meal once after they had surgery."

"Yeah." Mom looked up. "I think it was Mrs. Kelsey."

"Mrs. Kelsey?"

"Yes. Why? What's going on?"

"Well, I happened to notice that her house is up for sale. Do you think she might have some odd jobs I could do?"

"Hmm." Mom sipped her brew. "That's a great idea. If she's trying to sell the house, she might need some work done on it. And even if she moves, the experience might lead to more business."

"Do you think we can talk to her this Sunday?"

"Sure. Why not?"

I sprinted up to my room and phoned Dev. "Guess what?"

"You thought of a brilliant way for me to get revenge on you for spilling bubbles on me?"

"What? No."

"Uh... You learned Resh finally deals Dragona a deadly blow in the next movie?"

My head dropped. When would this Resh infatuation end? "No, but something nearly as good."

* * *

Mom pointed out Mrs. Kelsey that Sunday. An elderly woman, she wore a neon-orange dress and had spiky, gray hair.

I approached her and introduced myself. "I heard your house is on the market," I said, jumping at the chance to learn more about 275 Hidden Path Drive.

"Mmm hmm." She nodded as she swallowed coffee. Some miniature sculptures that dangled from her ears swung back and forth. "I've only lived here for five years, and now I'm moving again."

"Why so soon?"

"Some new apartments just went up near my daughter's house in Florida, and I'd like to move closer to her. I made an offer on one, but it fell through. It's too bad. I even had a job lined up teaching tap dancing to seniors." After handing me her coffee, she performed a kick ball change and made some jazz hands.

My eyebrows shot up. I hadn't been to a ballet class since preschool, and even then, I'd put up a fight about going. This woman, though, apparently still held onto a dream of making it as a prima ballerina.

"Now I'm looking to get something by early next year." Mrs. Kelsey took back her coffee and sighed.

"I hope everything works out for you." I pasted a polite smile on my face. I needed to get into her house.

"I hope so, too. But my agent here predicts doom." She extended her arm in a dramatic, helpless fling. "Houses in the area aren't moving at the moment, not in this economy."

I nearly rolled my eyes at her melodramatic gesture but stopped myself and forced my sneer into another smile. "If you need any help, I'd like to be the first to apply. I can rake leaves or do odd jobs."

"Impressive, but what I really need is someone who can cut the grass. A neighborhood girl used to do it, but she left for college this fall. I tried doing it myself these past few weeks but can't keep it up." Mrs. Kelsey shook her head, sending her sculpture earrings slamming into her cheeks. "Several lawn services have stopped by. They want so much money, though. And their roaring, fume-spewing equipment gets on my nerves. I much prefer my push reel mower."

"I could certainly give it a try." I stood up a little straighter.

Mrs. Kelsey sized me up. "You could probably handle it. My yard's not very big. Why don't you stop by tomorrow?"

Right after school Monday, I raced to Hidden Path Drive on my bike. I practically burst as I pedaled. Realistically, I didn't expect to find anything, especially with Mrs. Kelsey there. However, I couldn't help hoping I'd at least spot evidence of a bomb shelter. Part of me also imagined stumbling upon a dusty treasure chest in the back of a closet or a mound of gems stashed at the bottom of a drawer. As I pedaled along, my head filled with visions of briefcases stuffed with bills, jewel-studded crowns, and vaults holding out-of-print comic books. Caught up in my dreams, I nearly ran into a toddler who had wandered a few steps into the street. A baby-sitter scooped him up as I swerved to the side.

After rounding countless bends, I finally arrived at Two Seventy-Five. Instead of looking ordinary, the house seemed to sparkle today. Its dandelions and cheery yellow paint practically glowed. It definitely harbored something magnificent.

I walked up to the front door and peered behind the bushes. A crack or uneven section in the foundation might point to a secret room or a hidden panel. I might even find the handle of a trapdoor. Only when a van approached did I snap out of it. Excited voices of announcers and background cheers from a crowd blared from its radio as it passed.

I rang the doorbell. A dog's barks greeted me. Mrs. Kelsey came to the door, followed by a yelping, jumping Boxer.

"Hello, Erin." Her warm voice welcomed me in. "I hope you're not afraid of dogs. This is Cocoa." She bent over to scratch the dog's ears. Bangles around her wrinkled wrist clinked together.

Practically drooling as much as Cocoa, I stepped into the entryway. As I gave the dog a pat, I stole a glance around the room. Considering the house hid a secret, I half expected to find flaming torches in wall sconces and fireplaces lined with gargoyles, if not gold-framed portraits with eyes that followed my every move.

Instead, I entered a sunny living room filled with cheery furnishings. Cutesy cross-stitched puppies and kittens hung from the walls. Lace-covered pillows rested on a flowery-patterned couch.

"Like I mentioned yesterday, the grass needs to be cut," Mrs. Kelsey said. "And we'll get to the mower in a minute. But before we go out, I'll show you around the house."

I nodded hungrily, still convinced I'd spot swiveling bookshelves or a bulge in a Persian rug indicating a hatch hidden underneath.

"As you get to know me, you'll see I like to hide things," Mrs. Kelsey continued. "And I love treasure hunts. In fact, I made one up so you'd get more familiar with the place."

I nodded again, hesitantly this time. Before I could question her, though, she handed me a scrap of paper. "Here's the first clue. See if you can figure it out."

I took the note from Mrs. Kelsey's veined hand. The paper shook as I unfolded it. Did she suspect I knew about the house's secret? Maybe by leading me on a treasure hunt, she hoped to get me to confess my real purpose in working for her.

Trying to stop my hands from trembling, I squinted to decipher her tall, shaky handwriting, which she'd penned in purple ink.

-- A frog in a tutu

I took a closer look, frowning at the word *tutu*.

"Go ahead." Mrs. Kelsey nodded vigorously, all the while tapping her feet to a Latin beat coming from the lower level. "Try to figure out where to search."

I did my best not to look nauseated while I studied the note again. Then I shook my head and shrugged. "Ummm?"

"Why don't you try to find some frogs in the house?" Mrs. Kelsey smiled and pointed up the stairs. "Then maybe it'll make sense."

"Okay," I agreed, though my tone reeked of doubt.

I headed upstairs. Visions of luxurious furnishings, chests

of jewels, and priceless stamp collections filled my head. But the clue only led to a dancing frog figurine on a shelf. Underneath it, though, I found another clue, and two more after it.

Every moment I could, I looked around, hoping to spot a portrait covering a secret door or a loose floorboard hiding family heirlooms. I couldn't search much, though, with Mrs. Kelsey on my heels.

"Well, go ahead," she said after I'd deciphered the last clue. "Look for your prize."

The word *prize* made my hair stand on end. Did she know about the geocaching clues? Avoiding eye contact, I poked around a closet until I found a small package wrapped in gold foil.

Mrs. Kelsey laughed like a little kid as I tore off the paper and found a Resh Renner yo-yo inside.

"This is for me?" I asked, noting her laughter. I took it for a good sign but still puzzled over why she'd hidden clues and a prize.

"Yes, of course!"

She seemed sincere, but I didn't have the guts to question her about the treasure hunt. Finally, I simply thanked her.

"Let's take a look at that mower," she then said.

The maraca music grew louder as we approached the lower level. We entered the TV room. With Mrs. Kelsey briskly leading the way, I only had a few seconds to scan it before she ushered me through a washroom and into the backyard.

A few minutes later I got to work cutting the overgrown grass. I scowled as I pushed the clumsy reel mower, which someone had painted fuchsia. I would have rather worked algebra problems. I also frowned at not having a chance to search for valuables or the bomb shelter. Opal's family had expanded it in the house they'd moved into. I needed to find a way to look for it without arousing Mrs. Kelsey's suspicions.

Reaching the edge of the yard, I turned the mower around. Uh-oh. Maybe I'd already discovered the treasure. Probably quirky old Mrs. Kelsey was in on the secret, and the yo-yo was the prize. My shoulders slumped as another thought struck me: Or as Dev liked to joke, the clues might only lead to someone's bird carvings or some prized tail feathers.

Half an hour later I stowed the mower in the shed. Even though small, dark buildings now made me shudder, I poked around inside. Besides some tools and lawn chairs, I only found a family of pink plastic flamingoes, though.

"Come in! You don't have to knock." Mrs. Kelsey's gravelly voice bellowed from the kitchen after I rapped on the window. I opened the back door to find her standing at the counter, her arms elbow deep in a mixing bowl.

My eyes grew wide, and I froze in place on the threshold. Next to Mrs. Kelsey on the counter lay a small heap of jewels, sparkling and glittering as they reflected sunlight streaming through the window.

Mrs. Kelsey looked in the direction I was staring. "Oh." She waved away my trance. "I always take off my jewelry while baking."

I pried my eyes off the counter. "I finished cutting the grass, Mrs. Kelsey."

Cocoa let out a friendly bark and bounded over.

"Terrific. My Realtor just called. He'd like to show the house tomorrow, so I'm glad you got the yard cleaned up. That'll be all for today, but can you come back another day this week?"

My breath caught in my throat. I hadn't found the fortune yet. I couldn't leave so soon. The syncopated beat of steel drums sounding from downstairs added to my restless state. "Uh," I managed in a strained voice.

"How about Thursday?"

Thursday? I'd have to wait three entire days. "Sure." I swallowed an urge to protest and forced myself to smile. At least I'd return.

Chapter 12

Dev had to go to his cousin's engagement party that evening, so I didn't even try to call him. I couldn't talk to him at lunch the next day, either. After loading my tray with Swiss chard soup and an edamame patty, I learned my prepaid lunch balance had dropped to zero. Mom had probably forgotten to add funds. Or maybe she'd run out. Whatever the reason, I joined the back of the cash line, waited for what seemed like longer than a Resh Renner chase scene, and then paid with my own money. By the time I sat down, I barely had a minute to wolf everything down before the bell rang.

"So, what happened yesterday?" Dev huffed later, in gym, as he and I jogged around the school grounds. "Did you find the treasure of the Knights Templar?"

"Uh, no," I said, between breaths. "Just a Resh Renner yo-yo."

"A what?"

I filled Dev in on Mrs. Kelsey's cutesy needlepoint, the bizarre treasure hunt, and everything else as we ran along the track and swerved with the other students around Ms. Mode. Bundled up in a faux fur hat and mantle straight out of the Siberian tundra, she struggled to catch up with a cart of books that had teetered out of control as she'd wheeled it across the parking lot.

"I peeked into a few rooms but then worked outside. With Mrs. Kelsey inside, I couldn't look around much. The house is pretty small."

"Bummer." Dev stopped to pull up his mismatched gym socks. "My cousins' house was the same. Come to think of it, that style of house has some funny little niches."

I raised my eyebrows at him as we filed into the gym.

After school Dev came over. "Isn't there a small bedroom upstairs?" he asked as he flipped through one of Marcus's *Contraption Construction* magazines. "At the top of the stairs?"

"Yeah. There's a guest room near the landing."

"I suppose it would be a guest room in Mrs. Kelsey's house." Dev sounded offended. "In my cousins' it was the boys' room. Anyway, there's an empty shaft in one of the walls in that room. In some of those split-levels, it's been made into a built-in cabinet. In others, it's a safe, or vault, in the wall."

"A vault? Like a place where you'd store riches?"

"Exactly. It's in the wall between the closet and the window."

"Hmm." I'd only glanced into the room, but I tried to picture it. "I think Mrs. Kelsey has paintings in there."

"In my cousins' house there's a vault on that wall, right next to the closet." Dev tore a page out of the magazine showing some kind of bubble machine and drew a sketch on it. "The shaft is between that bedroom and the front door area, half a level lower. The closet by the front door fills most of the space in the shaft, but there's half a level of space above it that's empty. In my cousins' house, it's a vault accessed in the bedroom."

"So, behind Mrs. Kelsey's artwork..."

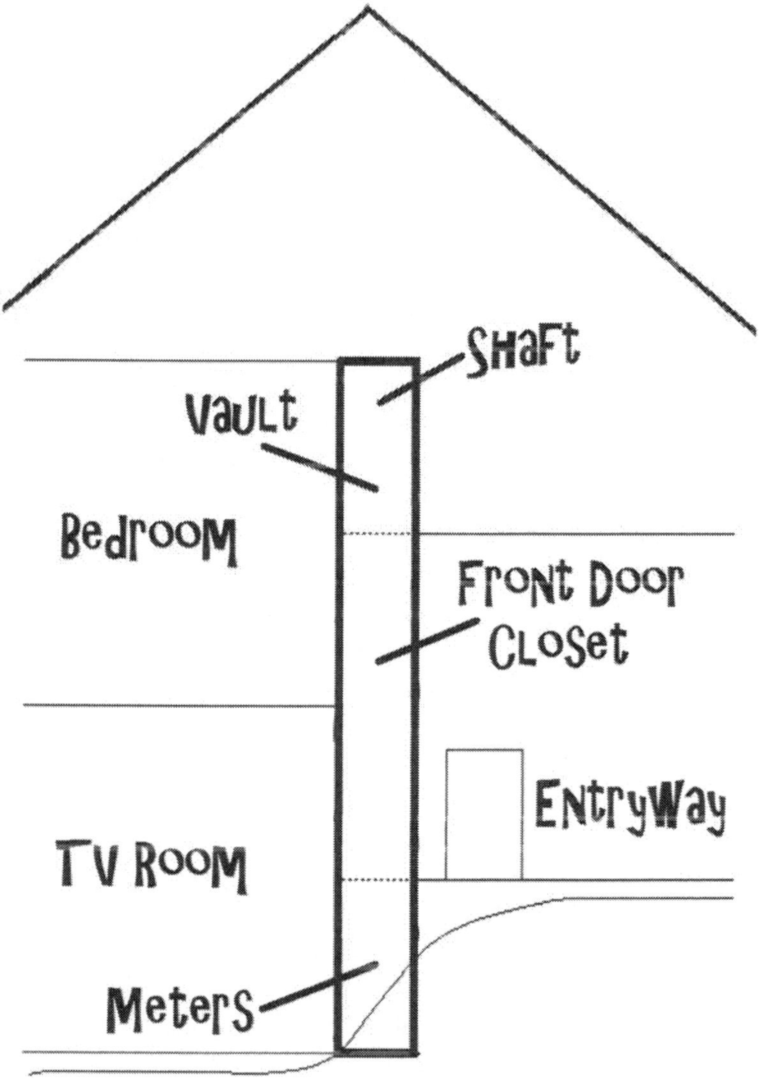
SHaFt
VauLt
Bedroom
Front Door
Closet
EntryWay
TV Room
Meters

"Thousands of doubloons await your discovery." Dev grinned like a ravenous beast who'd just spotted dinner. Sucking up his slobber, he added a few lines to his diagram. "Directly below the bedroom, or half a story down from the front door, is the TV room. There's empty space in the wall there, too, in the area underneath the front door closet. In the TV room, that space is near the floor and is usually filled with gas and electric meters."

I thought back to the previous day but shook my head. "Mrs. Kelsey led me through that room pretty quickly."

"Maybe she didn't want you to see the shaft." Dev let out a hiccup and released one of Marcus's Resh Renner magnetic darts. It flew across my desk, scattering algebra papers.

"What could she know about the Hamiltons, though?"

"What could anyone else know about them, including us? Yet we've come this far."

I frowned. "Rather Be Fishing might know something. He tried to run us over in that neighborhood."

"We need to figure out this thing, pronto." Dev let out a hiccup and released another dart.

* * *

I raced over to Mrs. Kelsey's after school Thursday. As I rounded a bend in Hidden Path Drive, I spotted a little kid again—the same one I'd seen Monday. This time, though, I got a better look at him.

His baby-sitter was wearing a baseball cap and blowing soap bubbles while also fiddling with a huge phone. The boy immediately burst the bubbles, letting out a scream with each pop.

As I biked past, the baby-sitter took off her cap. I nearly ran into a tree at the side of the road when her unbelievably long hair then spilled down her back.

Before me stood Fife & Drum with her receiver in hand. I swerved away from the tree just as she asked, "Go for a ride around the block?"

I stepped up my pace. My thoughts accelerated, too. If Fife & Drum was on to the mystery, she might have read through the profiles of all the geocachers who had picked up a wooden box. If she recognized me from the picture on Water Break's profile or remembered me from Suburban Obstacle Course, she might suspect my involvement. Worse, if she spotted me at the house, she might figure out the clues led there, without having read a single page of the diary.

I pedaled furiously toward Two Seventy-Five. She'd said something about going around the block. She must be tailing me.

The roar of a lawn mower filled my ears as I skidded past a parked white van and into Mrs. Kelsey's driveway. A tractor mower was combing the neighbor's yard. I hurried past it and hid my bike behind the house. Just as I ran for the front door, the clamor came to a stop.

"Hey, there!" a friendly voice called out from the mower.

I turned to find a middle-aged man lumbering toward me.

"Welcome to the neighborhood!" he shouted from halfway across the lawn.

"Oh, I don't live here." I shook my head. "I'm just working for Mrs. Kelsey." I scanned the street for a sign of Fife & Drum. Any second now, she would appear around the closest bend.

"Welcome anyway. I'm Steve Fogarta." The man grasped my hand in a firm shake.

Though still on the lookout for Fife & Drum, I couldn't help taking in the man's appearance. His long narrow face, which ended in a pointy chin, contrasted with his kind and twinkly Santa Claus eyes. His massive physique would have filled out Santa's suit, too. It looked solid, though, not plump and squishy.

"I take care of several lawns in the neighborhood," he continued.

"Nice to meet you." A stroller came into view around the bend. I crouched down, pretending to tie my shoe.

"So you landed the job at the Kelsey's," Steve went on. "I could never convince her to hire me." He shook his head.

I needed to get inside before the stroller got any closer. "I must have been in the right place at the right time." Praying the distance would prevent Fife & Drum from recognizing me, I stood up and turned to go into the house.

"Just like the Hulk's new quarterback." Steve grinned. "Did you hear that story? He's got a multimillion dollar contract. I bet you twenty bucks he'll lead them to victory this weekend."

"I hope they win, too." I mustered as much enthusiasm as I could as I peered around Steve's ample frame. The stroller was rounding the last bend.

"Anyway, keep an eye on the lady for me, will you? How's she doing these days? Still in good health?"

"Yes, I think so." I shifted my position and tried to hide behind Steve. I felt bad not engaging in the conversation. He'd bothered to ask about Mrs. Kelsey even after she'd apparently turned down his landscaping talents. But I couldn't risk letting Fife & Drum see me. Noticing her fast approaching with what looked like a small, armored tank, I ducked down and pretended to rummage through my backpack.

"You tell her I say hello." Steve flashed another grin.

"You bet." I offered the man a tenuous smile but stole another glance in Fife & Drum's direction. She must have meant business with that tank. Not wasting any time, she planned to unearth the mystery of 275 Hidden Path Drive immediately.

"And watch out for that ferocious dog, Cocoa!"

"Right." I exhaled. The tank turned out to be a toy. Spinning its miniature steering wheel, the kid made engine noises as his feet scooted the contraption along the street.

Still crouched over, I edged along the driveway until Mrs. Kelsey's chocolate-brown subcompact hid me from the street. After waiting for Fife & Drum to pass, I sprinted to the front door.

* * *

"First, a treasure hunt," Mrs. Kelsey announced as soon as I had crossed the threshold. She held out a folded-up scrap of paper. "My doctor says puzzles keep my brain fit."

I took the note but stared all the while at Mrs. Kelsey, trying to read her thoughts. Did she suspect me? If running into Fife & Drum's tank had unhinged me, then the treasure hunt clues completely disassembled me. I felt as spooked as if I'd wandered into a cave and found myself surrounded by gleaming eyes.

Warily, I unfolded the paper and read through the wobbly purple script. I exhaled, though, when Mrs. Kelsey retreated to a pottery wheel in the kitchen. I also glanced around. Without her hovering over me, I might search the vault or the meter storage Dev had talked about. As an added bonus, the kid might get bored with his tank before I got to the yard work.

As the pottery wheel whirred and hummed, I raced upstairs to the vault room. I scanned every inch of the wall, lifting up paintings and knocking everywhere. But instead of a hidden panel, I only stirred up dust and cobwebs.

Downstairs, I found the miniature door Dev had mentioned. Tucked away in the far wall, its narrow opening looked like it might even lead to a bomb shelter. Behind it, though, I only found a gas meter and a box overflowing with tiaras—plastic ones. Worse, through a cracked window I'd just heard a toddler roaring like a tank's engine. Fife & Drum had come to demand my surrender.

"Any luck on those clues?" Mrs. Kelsey suddenly appeared behind me.

I shook my head. I wanted to keep searching her house but couldn't risk alerting her suspicions.

"Take a look in here." She pointed toward the kitchen, where she provided a few improvised hints that led to a baseball.

"Thanks, Mrs. Kelsey." I tried to smile to hide my disappointment. I needed to find the Hamilton fortune, not a piece of cork wrapped in twine and horsehide.

"How about some raking today?" Mrs. Kelsey looked up from her pottery. "The maple trees have dropped so many leaves. You'll find a rake hanging in the shed."

"I'll get right to it." I tried to sound enthusiastic. My growing gloom dampened both my spirits and tone, though. In contrast, a little kid's fired-up imitation of tank artillery rang through the air as I opened the back door. I decided to tackle the backyard first to avoid Fife & Drum and the battle scene.

Half an hour later, I finally entered the front, where the

slightest breeze made me jump. But I might as well have worried that the authorities would soon outlaw toy tanks. Only two vehicles made their way down the street. First, Steve the gardener loaded up his equipment and drove away from the neighbor's yard. Seeing me struggling with the leaves, he stopped and lent me a bag holder. Then, just as I turned back to the raking, a delivery truck pulled up to the driveway.

When a burly woman got out and unloaded a large package from the truck's rear, Steve stopped again and dashed over to help her carry the box up the driveway. I wondered if he also lifted cans for the garbage men and helped the Girl Scouts deliver cookies. It sounded like he was now joking with the driver. Most likely he never missed a chance to discuss the Hulks and their last-minute, game-saving plays.

Steve's phone rang just as they reached the front door. "What's he talking about?" he yelled into it. "I paid him his fair share, according to the original agreement." He walked away, gesturing wildly. I put down the rake and jogged over to help the woman.

She held out a digital signature pad. "Sign Anne Kelsey," she ordered in broken English.

"Yeah, she's right here." I turned to get Mrs. Kelsey, but the woman, whose badge read, "Uda," shoved the device into my hands. When she gave me a stern look, I took the stylus and penned my own signature on the screen.

I then bent down to pick up the box but stopped short when the woman wagged her head at me and shook the digital device in my face. "I deliver," she said and snatched the box out of my reach.

Before she could smack me with the stylus, I jumped out of the way and held the door open for her.

As if on a mission, she then bulldozed straight into the house.

"Upstairs?" she barked as Mrs. Kelsey appeared in the entryway, her hands and face smudged with clay.

"Yes," Mrs. Kelsey answered, smearing clay into her hair, too. "That must be my new computer. And that would be a big help if you don't mind carrying it up into the guest room." She gestured toward the staircase. "Erin, maybe you could give her a hand."

I turned to help Uda with the box while Mrs. Kelsey went downstairs to get her vacuum cleaner. "I need to tidy up before I crawl around on the floor connecting all those cables," she explained.

Uda lifted the box on her own, though. When I tried to help her, she warded me off with a grunt and another shake of her head. She then marched toward the stairs.

I stepped back from her robust frame and let her pass. Generally I found it best not to get in the way of people with biceps as hefty as bowling balls, especially considering my own unsubstantial arm muscles. I gave them a poke. They seemed about as firm as deflated beach balls.

Hearing Mrs. Kelsey in the kitchen, wrestling with a ripped and overstuffed vacuum cleaner bag, I remembered my mission of searching the house. I raced upstairs.

In the guest room, I found Uda peering behind a painting hanging on the wall between the closet and the window — the vault wall. She gave a slight start when I entered. Then she replaced the frame on the wall, mumbling something about the picture getting scratched by the box.

How she'd managed to scratch the painting with cardboard, I couldn't fathom. And delivery people didn't usually stop to admire art, especially not pictures like this one, which didn't look at all out of the ordinary. Mrs. Kelsey might have painted it herself.

I didn't have time to investigate, though. A second later, Mrs. Kelsey schlepped her vacuum cleaner into the room and showed us both to the door. "If you can come back next Monday, I'm sure I'll have more work by then." She handed me my pay.

"Sure." I tried to hide my unease. Though I'd escaped Fife & Drum, I still hadn't found the Hamilton fortune. Worse, I'd caught Uda looking more suspicious than Marcus stealing money from the Resh-opoly bank.

* * *

I texted Dev to meet me at the ballpark right away.

"I ran into Fife & Drum on the way over to the Hamilton house," I said a little while later, as we tossed a ball back and forth. "And I found some tiaras."

"Some what?"

"They just turned out to be some old costumes. I think Mrs. Kelsey used to dance with a ballet company."

Dev threw me the ball, picked up a bat, and motioned for me to pitch. "What happened with Fife & Drum?"

"She was baby-sitting near the house and kind of followed me there." I wound up and threw, but Dev had no chance of connecting with the ball. I'd put it way outside.

He picked it up and returned it. "Did you find the vault?"

I threw another wild pitch. "No. I looked, but Uda was in there, too."

"Uda?" Dev retrieved the ball again.

"A delivery woman who brought something to the house and looked behind a painting." I scratched the back of my head. "She said she was just straightening the picture, though."

Dev lowered the bat. "Let me get this straight. Fife & Drum now knows about the house. Also, you couldn't find the vault, but someone else did?"

I tossed the ball up in the air and then caught it again. "That about sums it up."

Dev let out a low whistle in response to this latest blow. Then he took off his cap and smoothed his hair. After a while he motioned for me to continue pitching.

Finally I settled into a rhythm and got a few good throws in. With only two players, though, our game didn't draw a sellout crowd. A white van did pull into the parking lot, however.

"Heads up!" a deep, friendly voice shouted a minute later. I spun around to find Steve the gardener. He stood in the outfield, about to return a ball to the mound.

"Hey, thanks!" I caught the ball.

"Who's that?" Dev asked from home plate, nodding toward the outfield.

"A guy I met at Mrs. Kelsey's. He cuts the grass in that neighborhood."

"Hey! Let's play ball!" Steve called out from the field.

When Dev nodded, I wound and threw. Dev swung, knocking the ball beyond left field.

For the rest of the afternoon, Steve fielded while Dev and I alternated pitching and batting. My worries forgotten, I barely noticed the time passing. The day even topped playing with my dad and Marcus. The athletic Dev could hit and throw much better than my little brother, who typically caught and returned around two of every ten balls I threw. And Steve put on an unbelievable show. Never running out of steam, he performed one flashy trick after another, catching pop flies with his cap and sliding in the grass when diving for long straight shots.

Finally, when darkness settled in, Steve picked up the last of the balls and brought them into home plate. "I'm outta here." He turned to go.

"Hey. Thanks," Dev called after him. "I guess you used to play?"

"Yeah, back in high school. It's fun to relive the glory days. I never had talent like you guys, though. You've got a good arm, kid." He pointed to me. "All right. I gotta get home and get showered before kickoff. The Hulks have a big game tonight. See ya."

I must have gazed at Steve with a silly grin on my face as he left the field because Dev hit me lightly on the head with his glove to jolt me back to reality. Still, I couldn't let go of the thought that Steve had seen some potential in me. Maybe I did have a shot at making the school team that spring. Topping everything, I had another chance to search Mrs. Kelsey's house. I'd found nothing today, but she'd asked me to come back on Monday.

Unbelievably, my outlook had brightened. Unfortunately, the good feeling didn't last.

Chapter 13

A raw November wind whipped at my face as I waited for the bus the following Monday morning while a cold, driving rain drenched my jeans.

Dev's mood, too, had grown stormier. "You might as well return the diary to the library," he grumbled between bites of poached orange roughy on a stick. "I don't think it's gotten us anywhere."

I opened my mouth to protest but couldn't come up with a counter argument.

Engulfed in a sour mood, I plodded through the hallway between classes at school. Besides Dev's gloomy aura, I also had loads of homework to deal with. All the teachers kept piling on projects and papers, trying to cram in as much material as possible before winter break. Only Mrs. Dearg announced a homework-free week due to multiple marching band competitions she and her husband had going on.

Mostly the mystery bothered me, though. I hadn't seen any sign of a bomb shelter at Mrs. Kelsey's, and the most valuable thing I'd found so far was the worn and nicked Resh Renner yo-yo she'd given me but only because Dev had offered me ten dollars for it.

Bracing myself for Mrs. Kelsey's *tiki* bar music, I trudged through the cold wind to 275 Hidden Path Drive that afternoon.

"Here you go." She handed me a clue as soon as I stepped inside. "Go ahead and look for it. I need to get my drums set up." She pulled some drumsticks out of a drawer. "I take lessons. Usually my teacher comes on Tuesday, but she also baby-sits and asked if she could come this afternoon instead."

I almost groaned at the thought of another treasure hunt, but then I caught myself. With Mrs. Kelsey banging away, I might actually make some progress on the real treasure.

Ten minutes later, I stamped my foot as a stick caught in my rake. I'd searched everywhere in the house but had found nothing. Then Mrs. Kelsey had put me to work cleaning up the rest of her leaves.

I managed to free the stick, and when Steve honked from his van, I looked up and waved. I shook my head, though, as I returned to the raking. I hadn't expected to discover a passageway to a magical land inside one of Mrs. Kelsey's wardrobes. Still, the fact that I'd gotten nowhere with the search left me feeling more crushed than the yard waste in Steve's leaf compactor. With Mrs. Kelsey always around, I'd never dig up anything in the house.

Then I remembered the closet by the front door. It lay directly below the vault wall. The space above it might be accessible from that closet.

A little while later, I took a break and let myself in the door. I heard Mrs. Kelsey tapping her feet, shaking a maraca, and counting. Her lesson must have started. Also, I'd noticed a strange car parked at her curb, presumably the drum teacher's.

"Just hanging up my coat," I explained when the drumming stopped and Mrs. Kelsey peered around the corner. "I got warm raking." Although the wind had grown chilly, I couldn't think of a more reasonable excuse for accessing the closet.

Mrs. Kelsey nodded as she did a body roll and resumed counting.

I opened the closet door. As I reached for a hanger, I looked up at the closet's ceiling but found a shelf blocking my view.

"Ole!" Mrs. Kelsey had started spinning around the room, clicking castanets as she twirled.

I stepped back, draped my coat around the hanger, and then peered up, beyond the shelf. An ostrich feather hat sat above it in a huge space that extended impossibly high up into the closet, much further than the ceiling of the entryway. Delicate, multicolored plumes stuck out of the hat at random angles, filling the entire upper end of the shaft.

When Mrs. Kelsey picked up a scarf and started shimmying in my direction, I closed the closet. Before she could recruit me as a dance partner, I let myself out the door.

* * *

As my rake cleared away the leaves, my mind mulled over what I'd seen. I could cross the upper end of the shaft off my list. The closet by the front door simply extended up into that space. The question of the bomb shelter still remained, though.

I gazed up at the house, probably raking three times over the same spot. With Mrs. Kelsey occupied inside, I might search for it now.

While she drummed away, I edged closer to the foundation. I even cleared all the leaves out of the shrubs circling the house just to search for secluded nooks, portals to other dimensions, or unusual looking mouseholes.

Aside from a few cracks and chips in the paint, though, I found nothing. Even in the back I had no luck as far as I could see. One small section I didn't inspect. Some perfumy bushes covered that spot, and I didn't feel like stinking like flowers for the rest of the day.

Once I'd tied up the last leaf bag and stacked everything at the curb, I headed back toward the house. The drum teacher's car caught my eye again. This time, however, I noticed a magnet on its back bumper. "Drummers live longer, 'cause they keep time," it read.

I stared at the car, wondering why those words sounded familiar. Then, like two gigantic cymbals clashing in my head, realization struck. Dev and I had seen that bumper sticker on Fife & Drum's car at the Steaming Cauldron cache.

Feeling more rattled than a cartoon character hitting a gong, I stared wide-eyed and open-mouthed at the car. Not only was Fife & Drum Mrs. Kelsey's drum teacher, she was in the Hamilton house at that very moment! And she visited it regularly.

I swallowed hard and stumbled over to the door. Inside, I overheard Mrs. Kelsey's voice. "Oh, I must have left that book upstairs. I was going over it yesterday while I was painting."

"I'll get it for you," a pretty voice said. "Stay put." From around the corner a woman with comically long hair emerged, drumsticks in hand. Seeing me, she waved hello. "It's in the guest room, I assume?" She sprang up the stairs, her hair grazing her behind with every step.

"Yes, I believe so," Mrs. Kelsey answered. She looked up. "Ah, hello, Erin."

Still in shock, I gaped at the staircase and gestured in a meaningless way. Mrs. Kelsey had let Fife & Drum into her home. And she did it on a weekly basis! Nothing would ever stop Fife & Drum from beating me to the prize.

"Uh... sorry to interrupt, Mrs. Kelsey," I finally managed to say. I stole furtive glances toward the staircase. "I finished the raking."

"Thank you, dear. I hope you'll come back on Thursday. Could you come in the evening instead? Usually I play Bridge Thursday evenings, but the group wants to meet in the afternoon this week."

"Uh, sure." I nodded, still feeling like I'd swallowed a drumstick.

"Great." She led me to the door. "Is something wrong, dear?" She frowned when I didn't follow. "You don't seem well."

"I'm fine," I squeaked. I craned my neck toward the guest room, where Fife & Drum lingered.

"Oh, your pay!" Mrs. Kelsey rummaged around for her purse. "Why didn't you say anything?"

"Uh... right." I'd probably turned green at that point, but I managed to pocket the money.

"I'm sorry, Mrs. Kelsey, but I can't find it," a voice yelled from upstairs.

"Oh, here it is." Mrs. Kelsey picked a music book up off the floor. "It must have slid off the stand during that last number." She turned back to me. "See you Thursday."

I felt like I'd been battered with a bass drum mallet. "Right. See you then." I slumped out the door.

* * *

Still picturing Fife & Drum prowling around Mrs. Kelsey's house, I called Dev as I pedaled home. He sounded more upset by the news than if he'd misplaced his Resh Renner sunglasses.

I couldn't go back until Thursday, though. So when the sun came out the next afternoon, Dev and I headed instead toward Mystery Hills Lake. We'd endured one of Mrs. Dearg's dizzying history exams that morning on Orellana and Pizarro's pursuit of El Dorado and needed to blow off some steam. More importantly, I'd just learned about a new cache hidden at the lake. Fife & Drum had planted it.

"Didn't Fife & Drum once write a log about 'winning the prize'?" Dev asked as we set out on a trail that circled the water.

"Yeah. That's why I wanted to check out her container and logbook."

Following the navigation directions, we hiked to the cache's site, a rocky area just off the path on the lake's far side.

"What is all this stuff?" Dev wondered. We'd found the cache under a slab of red shale. He sifted through some shoulder pads in the container and a pair of pants with elastic stirrup straps attached near the ankles. Next he pulled out what looked like long, knitted socks without feet. "Maybe I can trade my Resh Renner binoculars for these yarn tubes." He stretched them onto his arms. "I've got at least another three pairs of Resh field glasses at home."

I grabbed the container. After poking through a few narrow leather ties, something labeled "Cassingle," and a sweatshirt with a ripped collar, I finally located the logbook. Trapped among water droplets inside a plastic bag, it smelled funky. I held my nose and thumbed through it. "It's an '80s-themed cache," I reported. "It says, 'Leave only '80s-related items.'"

"Eighties stuff? Meaning these arm sweaters are actually leg warmers?" Dev held up his arms and drew his head back, shrinking away from the sight of them. Grasping the edge of the fabric with a thumb and the tip of a finger, he pulled them off. "I think I'll hold onto my binoculars."

I didn't laugh. Dev already looked as embarrassed as if his mom had delivered his Resh Renner lunchbox to the school office and told him over the announcements to pick it up. "We can still log the find," I offered in consolation instead. "But there's no other info in the logbook. There's nothing about Fife & Drum or her quest for the prize."

Dev and I exchanged grim looks. I stashed the container back under the shale, and we strolled over to the lake.

We sat down on a boulder near the shore. I tossed a rock into the water, where it landed, kerplunk, with a lake-shattering splash. "I wonder why Fife & Drum set up the cache."

Dev hurled a large rock far into the lake but didn't answer.

"I mean, if she really wanted to find the fortune, why would she take the time to hide a container filled with '80s stuff?" I searched the ground until I found a perfectly smooth, flat stone. With a flick, I released it. As I watched, it skipped across the water, jumping once, twice, maybe three times before disappearing into the ripples.

"Maybe she planted it as a trap." Dev skipped his own stone across the lake.

His comment gave me goosebumps. I scanned our surroundings. But aside from a solitary guy fishing near the dock, the scene looked as secluded and serene as a remote island hiding long forgotten treasure.

"Or maybe it's just a diversion." Dev threw more stones and branches into the lake, disrupting its sleepy waters.

"What do you mean?" I picked up a twig and doodled in the mud.

Dev threw a globe-sized rock into the waves. Then he jumped back when it made a huge splash. "Maybe she lured us here so she'd have time to bind and gag Mrs. Kelsey, then search her house." He shook out his hair and brushed off his clothes. "Or maybe the clues just lead to a collection of bird's nests and eggshells salvaged from the Hamiltons' barn."

I rolled the stick back and forth between my hands as I considered his ideas. Then a flash across the lake caught my attention. The fisherman we'd seen earlier was waving something metallic in the bright sunlight. He'd packed up most of his gear and now stood next to a cooler, brandishing the shiny object. Occasionally he gazed over at Dev and me.

"Dev, do you see that man over there?" The guy's odd behavior gave me a bad feeling.

"Yeah." Dev let a rock drop to the mud. "Hold on. Let's get a better look." He crouched down behind a tree and pulled out the binoculars he'd almost traded for a pair of leg warmers. After adjusting the focus, he zeroed in on the man. "He's sharpening a knife. A big knife. And he's looking this way."

"Let me see." I joined Dev behind the tree. My mouth went dry as the man came into focus. "That's Rather Be Fishing."

"No way!" Dev grabbed the spy gear and peered

through the lenses. "You're right! What's he doing here with that knife? And why does he keep staring at us?"

"A few weeks ago he nearly ran us over with his pickup." My pulse rate quickened.

"But he stopped short," Dev pointed out, "since we were out in the open, on a residential street."

"Exactly. I'm sure he wanted to hurt us but just decided to wait for a better opportunity." Looking around at our secluded surroundings, I realized the lake would make an ideal spot for a violent crime.

Apparently Dev had the same thought. "Why do you think he brought the cooler?" he asked. "You don't suppose he's the type to chop us to pieces, then preserve our body parts for some gruesome, post-murder ceremony?"

"You didn't have to mention that last part." I took one more look through the binoculars. Again I caught Harold staring in our direction.

Dev and I scrambled back into the woods, away from the bank.

"Which way?" Dev asked. He snapped his fingers repeatedly. "The trail we took here will just bring us back near the dock and Harold."

"The other direction also leads to the dock." I bit my lip. "It makes a loop." Consulting the app, I switched into map mode and zoomed out. "Look, there's a street just beyond the woods here." I pointed to a road displayed on the screen. "If we continue down the trail for another tenth of a mile, then cut through the woods, we'll reach the houses in that neighborhood. We should be safe there."

We set off at a sprint. After a minute I checked the screen. "Let's break off here."

I led the way into the woods. In this new terrain, with its branches and tangled undergrowth, we moved about as quickly as Marcus did when hiking through a woods teeming with interesting distractions. We muddled our way through bushes, leaves, and low branches for several minutes while dodging trees, stumps, and thorns. Then we heard tires squealing in the distance.

"Was that Harold's truck?" Dev's voice came out higher than usual. "Maybe he saw us race off. Do you think he'll park in that neighborhood and try to intercept us?"

I checked the screen. "Only three tenths of a mile until we reach the street." I tried not to think of Harold or his sharp knife.

We tore through the jungle of plants. Prickly branches snapped back and caught on my hair and jacket as I passed. Still, we kept going, bushwhacking through the dense vegetation for several more minutes. Finally the trees thinned. We saw the outline of something red ahead, a house maybe. Not caring if we were trespassing on private property, we burst through the last few feet of trees, landing in someone's backyard. We panted and clutched stitches in our sides while we raced on to the front and the street. There we paused for a minute to catch our breath.

Although we didn't see a sign of Harold, we continued at a jog. Brakes squeaked somewhere. Then tires squealed. Dev and I ran for cover in a hedge. When Harold failed to materialize, we stepped out but quickened our pace.

When a white van pulled up right behind us, I nearly scurried up a tree before I realized Steve sat behind the wheel.

"Hey." Steve rolled down the window.

"Steve!" I said, still catching my breath. "So glad to see you."

"What's up with you two?" Steve looked from me to Dev. "You look like you just saw a ghost." He handed us a pizza box from the passenger seat. "Here, have a slice."

"We were at Mystery Hills Lake," Dev said, helping himself. "And this guy came after us with a knife."

"What!?"

"We're not sure he actually chased us," I explained. "But this fisherman kept staring at us and waving a huge knife. And he tried to run us over with his truck a few weeks ago."

"W-What!?"

"Yeah. We found some clues leading to Mrs. Kelsey's house," Dev said. "We think maybe he knows about them, too, and wants us out of the way."

"Clues?" Steve turned down the radio. "Mrs. Kelsey's house?" He scratched his pointy chin. For the first time, I noticed a deep crease in his brow.

"Yeah. Why? Is that your territory?" Dev joked.

"It is," Steve answered, smiling. "Except for the small patch at Two Seventy-Five. I've been trying for years to become king of that hill, but Erin, here, beat me to it." Steve winked at me.

Still feeling freaked, I barely smiled.

Steve's grin faded at my muted reaction. The crease on his brow also reappeared. "Did you guys call the police?"

"No." I shook my head. "We're not sure he followed us. We've just been running since we saw him, trying to get away."

"Anyway, he's gone by now. We heard his truck racing off." Dev finished off the last of his crust and wiped his hands on his jeans. "Thanks, Steve."

"No problem. Another slice?"

Dev looked tempted, but I tugged on his arm. "We've got to go."

Finally we reached Dev's house, where the rich smell of his grandma's cooking greeted us.

His dad welcomed me in. Before we could say anything about Harold or his knife, Dev's mom even invited me to stay for dinner. She and Mr. Johar kept up a steady stream of questions, and Dev's sisters and grandma kept sneaking peeks at me while we ate.

I could see why Dev complained about their nosiness. But I didn't mind. Dev had a family—a big, warm, friendly family. They made me feel so much at home, I nearly forgot the drama at the lake.

Chapter 14

That evening, I tried working on an essay on Francisco Coronado's search for the Seven Cities of Gold. Concentrating proved about as easy as bushwhacking through granite, though.

From the top of a stack of books, my phone beckoned. I picked it up and opened a text window.

Erin: Uncle El? You there?

Uncle El: Always.

I shook my head. I swore his response had arrived before I'd hit *Send*.

Erin: Scared & tired.

The spine-tingling brush with Rather Be Fishing at the lake still haunted me. My head tilted to the side.

Erin: Confused, too.

I paused for a minute to gather my thoughts.

Erin: I'm glad to work for Mrs. Kelsey. No complaints there. First I thought she'd lost her marbles. Now she's fun & pay is great.

My head dropped.

Erin: I don't mean to be greedy, but

I let out a long sigh.

Erin: I'm not making progress on mystery. The diary only leads to dead ends.

The tiaras came to mind, as did the pile of jewelry in the kitchen. And the other day I'd come across some gilded books and a closet full of bright gold sculptures. I'd thought I'd stumbled upon priceless treasures, until Mrs. Kelsey mentioned she'd recently discovered the joy of spray glitter. She'd bought several cans on sale at a wholesale market and was coating everything in sight with gold sparkles, including books and plastic figures she'd found at garage sales.

Erin: So bummed. Feel like I'm in toilet bowl.

The whole situation made me think of a slide at a nearby water park. It had a round section called the toilet bowl, where the incline leveled out. Inner tubes often got stuck there. Like someone trapped in that basin, drifting to and fro, I saw no way of moving forward.

Erin: And Dev's down. Today he said if something's buried, he doesn't know how we'd get to it.

My forehead hit the desk.

If I didn't solve the mystery before someone else did, I would never earn a reward. Without money, I had no hope of reuniting my family. My dad would return from Hawaii soon but would then land a new job in some other remote place, leaving Marcus, Mom, and me to rot in our bleak, concrete-embedded apartment.

A beep jolted me back to the present. Uncle El had e-mailed a link to an online video. I clicked on it, wondering if he had posted a movie of himself singing karaoke or performing stand-up comedy. The black and white footage showed people getting splashed on a water ride, though. It looked familiar. I hit *Play* again and squinted at the screen. A sign in the background said Toilet Bowl Exit.

He'd sent a video of the ride with its steep slope that led to a big splash at the finish. Even if you got stuck in the bowl, eventually the water flushed you down the pipe, shooting you out of the tunnel and down to the exit.

I replayed it and gazed at the people in the inner tube. Some laughed. Some pumped their fists. Others waved at the camera or flashed a thumbs-up.

I leaned back in my chair. The mystery of how Uncle El had acquired the water park's security tape didn't faze me. He had numerous sources and connections who provided him with inexplicable amounts of information. Instead, I felt like someone had patted me on the back. In place of fruitless searches and pointless dead ends, I pictured the drop-off at the end of the ride that guaranteed everyone finished sopping wet but smiling.

Erin: Maybe there is something hidden at the house.

The fact that Rather Be Fishing chased us could mean we still had something to search for.

Erin: That doesn't make it easier to find or guarantee Fife & Drum won't find it first. But I'll keep looking.

Maybe I'd soon solve the mystery. Or, if not a breakthrough, tomorrow might at least bring fewer encounters with thorn-covered plants and knife-wielding fishermen.

Erin: Over & out.

* * *

Finally Thursday arrived, and I could resume my quest for the Hamilton fortune. The fact that Fife & Drum visited Mrs. Kelsey's on a regular basis had kept me awake at night. Probably she'd already robbed the place bare while pretending to teach *salsa* moves. Still, until I got some answers, I wouldn't stop looking. In fact, as soon as Mrs. Kelsey let me take a break, I'd ask her to play something on her drums. While she banged away, I would then check all the closets, cabinets, and cobwebs, leaving nothing unturned until I made some progress.

My mom drove me over since she didn't want me biking in the dark. My foot tapped against the car floor the entire ride. As we turned into Hidden Path Drive, a white van approached from the opposite direction. I waved, recognizing Steve in the driver's seat. Maybe he'd play ball with us again soon. I might get enough practice in to make the school team.

"Who's that?" Mom asked.

"Steve. He does the landscaping for Mrs. Kelsey's

neighbors." I tried to catch Steve's attention again. But with both hands on the wheel he didn't see me as he drove past. Probably a Hulk's game on the radio had distracted him.

"It's a little dark for yard work." Mom glanced up at the sky.

"I guess someone kept him working late." I felt a tinge of pity for the guy.

At last we pulled up to Two Seventy-Five. "Where's your car?" I asked Mrs. Kelsey as she let me in. I hadn't seen her chocolate subcompact in the driveway.

"It gave me trouble after Bridge this afternoon, so it's in the shop. They'll look at it tomorrow."

After a treasure hunt that ended in a foam football covered with teeth marks, Mrs. Kelsey kept me busy cleaning out her attic. My first trip up the ladder, I imagined discovering a gold-filled chest buried under boxes of old photos or nestled among a maze of dusty, upturned furniture. The thrill fizzled when I only found pink storage bins filled with ponchos and bell-bottoms.

I waited and waited for Mrs. Kelsey to announce a break as I carried bins up and down the ladder. She must have forgotten about me, though. Cocoa did an excellent job of distracting her. Cocoa wouldn't stop growling the entire time I schlepped the bins. She woofed up into the attic hatch when I returned them to storage and tore back and forth through the house when I came down the ladder.

"What's wrong?" Mrs. Kelsey asked her for the zillionth time. She looked up from sorting through a pile of beehive wigs and men's extra large underwear.

A scuffling sound from below startled us. We looked at each other.

"It's really windy," I said. "Maybe a branch fell on the house. I'll go take a look."

I also thought about making a detour and peeking in a

kitchen closet I'd never investigated. As I headed downstairs, though, a loud clang rang out from the living room. Hurried footsteps then issued from the kitchen.

My heart hammered faster than a snare drum gearing up for a roll. Someone was in the house.

Taking the steps three at a time, I sprang into the kitchen. "Who's there?"

A figure in a dark coat dashed away across the backyard.

I sprinted out the sliding door and ran onto the lawn but didn't see anyone. When I heard tires squealing in the street, I scrambled to the front. By the time I got to the road, though, I could only make out two red taillights disappearing around the nearest bend in the curvy road. Panting, I paused for a moment to catch my breath and staggered back to the kitchen.

* * *

"What's up with you?" Dev whispered across the aisle in history class the next morning. Mrs. Dearg had just taken a break from her lecture on Juan Ponce de Leon's pursuit of riches in the New World to pass out some worksheets. "You look like you barely slept."

"I was at Mrs. Kelsey's until late last night." I grabbed a sheet from the stack but ended up with more than one. Without even putting the extras back, I passed the rest along. "Someone broke into the house while we were there."

"No way!"

"Yeah. But they got away. It took forever to deal with the police afterwards—"

"Ms. Schmidt and Mr. Johar, we are discussing pre-colonial explorers." Mrs. Dearg did not look like she was about to announce another homework-free week.

"Unless you care to elaborate on Ponce de Leon's gold-seeking expeditions in Puerto Rico, I suggest you hold your comments until after class." Her frizzy red hair grazed the padded shoulders of her '80s blazer with every syllable.

Dev missed lunch since he had to make up a spores and fungi lab. But as soon as band started, he peppered me with questions. "A break-in? What were you doing there at night? Did they take anything?"

"Yes, there was a break-in." I grabbed my flip stand as the class headed outside for marching practice. "But no, I don't think they took anything. Or at least Mrs. Kelsey didn't think so. Her living room shelves were ransacked, though."

"Did you see what they looked like?" Dev slurped up some drool as he hooked his bass drum to his harness. He sounded as excited as if he'd finally accessed the time portal in Resh's latest video game.

"No. They heard me coming and ran."

"How'd they get in?" Dev joined the other drummers at the front of the group.

"Through the sliding door in back." Hoping to continue the conversation, I sneaked up to the trumpet section, right behind the drummers, as we began circling the field. "Somehow they disengaged the door guards. Apparently they thought no one was home at first, because Mrs. Kelsey's car was in the shop, not in the driveway. She usually goes out on Thursday nights, but last night she was home."

"It sounds like the burglar knew her schedule." Dev stood up straighter and tried to hide me behind his drum as we passed Mr. Weber.

"Exactly. And this wasn't the first time either. The officer mentioned something about past incidents at the house."

"Wow. Maybe there really is something hidden there." We marched with the others for a minute. Then Dev missed a beat. "I bet it was Fife & Drum. She must know Mrs. Kelsey's schedule if she sets up a drum lesson every week. Plus, you saw her poking around the guest room."

"Right." I ducked as Mr. Weber turned in our direction. "But she was actually friendly when I saw her, not at all cagey. Also, there's another problem."

"What's that? Hold on a sec." Dev grabbed my arm as we passed the bleachers. He pulled me through the gap between two sections and led the way underneath the seats.

I glanced around, hoping Mr. Weber wouldn't notice we'd left the group.

Dev kept tugging me along and then unhooked his drum and plopped down on the ground. "What's the other problem?"

I took a seat next to him. "I checked her profile late last night, and the picture shows two people. It's a dim, faraway shot, but neither of them have long hair. I think one's even a redhead. They both look bulky and broad shouldered, like they're wearing shoulder pads, or something."

"Strange. But why was she watching us when we dropped off Magpie?"

"Anyone would have stared at two kids snooping around prickly bushes in a parking lot. I bet it was just a coincidence that she followed us when we dropped off Magpie. Isn't there a music store in that strip mall?"

"Um, yeah," Dev admitted. "But maybe she just put up a random picture on the profile, so no one would be able to identify her."

"Possibly, but there are two other problems."

Twirling a mallet, Dev nodded for me to continue.

"Mrs. Kelsey's drum teacher has been giving her lessons for a few years, and The Bird Watchers just launched the music boxes a month ago. That woman started coming to her house long before the mystery came up."

"Okay."

"Also, the fife part is missing. She's just a drummer."

"Hmmm." Dev tapped the drum with his fingers. "Something doesn't jibe, though. Didn't you see Fife & Drum in Mrs. Kelsey's neighborhood just a few weeks ago?"

"Yes. And I thought she was following me to the house."

"Ha." Dev tapped my knee with his mallet and gave me a look that clearly said, "Got you there."

"She wasn't after me, though. Read the logs if you want proof. She checked on the cache by the lake that afternoon since there had been complaints about the container being wet."

"Oh." Dev tossed the mallet up in the air.

I wagged my head. "I still think it was Rather Be Fishing. Remember? We saw his truck in her neighborhood recently. He's probably been scoping out the scene."

Dev tilted his head from side to side, weighing my comments. "He did try to attack us at the lake."

"Exactly. He must know we're searching, and he's trying to eliminate the competition."

"But what about Uda?" Dev tossed the mallet again.

"She did poke around the guest room." I grabbed the mallet when Dev started tapping on my knee again. "Maybe she also thinks there's something hidden in the vault."

"Definitely suspicious behavior. I don't think delivery people are supposed to enter houses."

"Plus, she let me sign for the package, instead of waiting for Mrs. Kelsey's signature." I remembered the digital signature pad and my fears of being whacked with it.

"Hmmm."

"Wait a second. We're forgetting something." I stood up as the band approached us on their second loop around the field. "No one else has seen Opal's diary. I just renewed it, and I can renew it again the middle of December."

"So no one else could know about the house." Dev hooked the drum to his harness. "Are you saying the break-in was just a coincidence?"

"I don't know." We slipped in with the woodwinds as they passed the bleachers. "But in case it wasn't, we'd better figure out this mystery soon, before someone else does."

* * *

Something burned inside me the rest of that day. I kept seeing the dark coat in Mrs. Kelsey's backyard and the taillights disappearing down the street. Someone else knew about the house's secret and had tried to get away with the prize. My innards smoldered over that fact.

The whole experience also put me on red alert. As soon as I got home, I counted my cash, afraid robbers had struck the apartment, too. I let out a sigh when I found it all there.

With the bills still in my hand, I looked up flights to Hawaii on a travel web site. My head dropped to my chest. My earnings wouldn't even buy me an off-peak, one-way ticket.

If I ever wanted to see Dad again, I either needed to get a job with an airline or make some progress on the mystery.

But by Thursday of the following week, I'd still turned up nothing new. I arrived at 275 Hidden Path Drive wondering if I should apply for a position restocking barf bags on 747s.

"I need help with my new speakers," Mrs. Kelsey explained as she led me downstairs. "My stereo system is all down here by the TV." She gestured toward some equipment sitting on a shelf in the TV room. "My drum set is upstairs, though, and sometimes I like to play along to music."

"Do you carry the set down here?" I pictured her descending the stairs with drums, music books, and a wire stand piled high in her arms, everything teetering out of control.

"No, no." She waved away my concern. "The set stays upstairs. I just bought an extra pair of speakers for that room. I need your help connecting them to the stereo down here. There are jacks for speaker wires in the walls, here and in the living room."

I yawned as I nodded to show I understood.

Her next comment woke me up pretty quickly. "I just want to run the wiring from this outlet down here through the crawlspace and up into the living room."

My head lurched at the word *crawlspace*. My knees also grew wobbly. I felt like I'd just raced down a mountain trail as a storm approached, overexerting my legs with each pounding step. "Did you say this house has a crawlspace?"

"Yes, there's a crawlspace behind this wall in the washroom. It extends back underneath the living room." Mrs. Kelsey pointed in that direction. "That's where I need your help. With my old, feeble bones and stiff hip, I can't move around in such a cramped space."

"Okay." I nodded. I also nearly kicked myself for not

considering the possibility earlier. A crawlspace could hide an entire spectrum of bedazzling treasures. My head buzzed with thoughts of overflowing chests, precious works of art, and DVDs holding never-before-aired Resh Renner episodes—for Dev, of course.

Misreading me, Mrs. Kelsey continued. "I know it's silly to run the wire now, when I'm planning on moving, but it may be a while before the house sells. Also, it's a straightforward job that could increase the property's value."

I smiled politely while trying not to salivate or pant.

"Let me show you the crawlspace door," Mrs. Kelsey said. "It's behind Cocoa's food."

Once inside the washroom, I helped her move several towers of dog food cans aside. On my hands and knees, I then crawled under some ductwork to reach the wall. It was covered with pink foam insulation panels.

"All but one of the insulation boards are screwed into place," Mrs. Kelsey directed from the washroom. "See if you can pry that one loose." She pointed to the board on my right. "Oh, and here, you'll need these." She pushed a flashlight and some tools in my direction. I removed the loose panel and set it aside, revealing the opening.

After switching on the flashlight, I wiggled my way into the crawlspace. Bolts of energy zipped along my spine. I might stumble upon the Hamilton's priceless baseball card collection right here, under the house.

Chapter 15

My hair stood on end as I looked around the space, which extended about thirty feet in either direction. Rubble covered the ground. Cobwebs drooped from the low ceiling. Dust hung in the air, visible in the flashlight's beam. Otherwise, though, it stood empty. Instead of chests full of glistening gems, the only thing that caught my attention was a faint, checkered light coming from a rectangular spot on the far wall.

I squinted at it, realizing it was a vent built into the foundation. But I hadn't noticed it earlier, when I'd searched the exterior. Suddenly I remembered the smelly bushes on that side of the house. I punched myself. If only I hadn't worried about smelling like flowery perfume, I would have found the crawlspace weeks ago.

"I just slipped the wire through the jack here in the TV room." Mrs. Kelsey's faint voice came from somewhere near the opening. "If you stay close to that wall, you should find it."

"Okay." I edged along the wall. After finding the wire, I turned around and advanced toward the far wall, securing the wire into the ceiling every few feet with some clips. Hearing a rustling sound, I scooted back, hoping I wouldn't spot a rat.

At last I reached the far wall. I searched for the opening, afraid I'd also find an entire family of rodents as I checked for holes in every shadow and indentation on the rough concrete.

Probing further, I stumbled as my foot caught on something sticking up from the ground. I spun around, hoping not to find a nest. A branch or root seemed to be jutting out of the concrete. I bent down to take a closer look. After brushing away lots of dust, I uncovered something metallic. I dug further, revealing a handle.

My heart pounded as I grasped it and pulled upward. Nothing budged. I leaned closer, locating a crevice in the ground nearby. Following the line of the gap, I brushed away more dirt. Soon, I'd exposed the rectangular frame of a door built into the ground.

Fireworks burst inside me. It might be a trapdoor leading to a bomb shelter. I felt as gaga as Dev over rumors of a new Resh movie coming out before year's end. I grabbed the handle and pulled harder.

It held fast.

Shifting my position and adjusting my grip, I crouched, poised to try again, when Mrs. Kelsey's voice sounded through the space.

"Erin, you need to come out now! Erin, your mom is here. We can finish the wiring job some other day."

"I'm right here, Mrs. Kelsey." I scrambled back to the wall, hoping she hadn't somehow detected me closing in on a big secret. Then I found the speaker wire opening. "I'm at the outlet. I'll put the wire through. Can you grab it?"

"Yes, but then come right out."

I shoved the end through the hole. With one last longing glance at the handle in the floor, I edged back toward the washroom.

My mom stood just outside the opening looking as frazzled as the time Marcus had used her slow cooker to simulate global warming in his terrarium. "Sorry, Erin, but we need to leave right away," she said. "I've got a budget crisis meeting at work this evening, and I need you at home with Marcus. I already loaded your bike into the back of my car."

I felt like the floor had shifted under my feet. I shot Mrs. Kelsey a pleading look, hoping she would protest my leaving early, giving me an excuse to reenter the crawlspace.

She smiled warmly but offered no help. "I can finish hooking the wires up to the speakers myself, Erin. I just needed you to get it through the jacks. At my age I can't get into the crawlspace. Thanks for all you've done. Can you come back next Monday?"

"But, what about... B-but," I stammered until my mom raised her eyebrows at me. "Yeah, sure, Mrs. Kelsey." I headed out to the car with Mom, my spirit more dampened than if I'd trudged through the rain for an hour.

As soon as we got home, Mrs. Kelsey called.

"Hi, Erin. I meant to ask you something before you left."

"Oh?" I grabbed a fistful of hair and twisted it. She must have sensed me snooping around her crawlspace.

"This just came up, but I'm leaving for Florida tomorrow for three days. Would it be too much to ask you to take care of Cocoa while I'm away? You'd have to feed her and walk her twice a day."

"N-Not at all, Mrs. Kelsey." I detangled my fingers from my hair. "I'd love to."

"Terrific. My daughter just phoned. A condominium opened up near her. It's only three months old, but the current owners are already moving out, their marriage gone awry. I'd like to take a look at it and maybe make an offer. I'll get you a key and leave some instructions."

The instant she hung up, I phoned Dev. "What are you doing tomorrow?"

"Getting revenge on you for spilling those bubbles on me?"

"What? Uh ... no."

"Then I'm flying to Hollywood with you, so we can pose as extras in the next Resh Renner film?"

"Aargh!"

"What?" Dev feigned innocence.

"No. We're not California bound. But something nearly as good."

* * *

I couldn't think straight at school the next day. Somehow I ordered a side of bok choy at lunch although the cafeteria actually offered baby carrots for once.

Finally classes ended. In spite of the fierce December wind, Dev and I biked over to 275 Hidden Path Drive.

"Maybe this whole search is one huge multi-cache," Dev shouted through his ski mask. We'd both pulled knit caps over our heads to keep Rather Be Fishing and Fife & Drum from tracking us down.

"What do you mean?" I waved to Steve as he passed in his van, all bundled up. I hoped he hadn't contracted frostbite while deadheading someone's roses.

"Remember the afternoon we spent tracking down Suburban Obstacle Course?"

"Yeah," I answered. "We couldn't figure it out until we found the hidden ladder."

"Exactly." Dev zigzagged down the empty street. "I bet this wooden box mystery is just a huge cache that we have to decrypt. Maybe there's even a ladder underneath that handle. One that leads to a crypt."

"Hmm." I tried not to think of decaying bodies and other cadaverous things crypts held.

We reached the house. "What's this?" Dev unfolded a note written in shaky purple handwriting.

-- Behind Cocoa's lair

I smiled. "Mrs. Kelsey always gives me clues leading to a prize. She must have hidden something in the crawlspace."

"Which gives us the perfect excuse to snoop around." Dev sprang down the stairs. "Let's get going."

In the washroom I found some flashlights and a crow bar in Mrs. Kelsey's tool chest. "We'll need something to pry open the trapdoor with." I pulled a gadget out of my pocket. "I also packed Marcus's Resh Renner voice-recorder, invisible-ink-decoder, lock-picker, just for fun." When Dev looked like he might spend all day inspecting it, I urged him on. Then I led the way into the house's dark, dirty recesses.

Once Dev had joined me, I aimed my flashlight at the far wall. "The trapdoor's over there."

"What's with Cocoa?" he asked over some yelps and barks.

"Don't worry, she'll calm down in a minute. She's probably jealous that she doesn't get to go exploring, too."

As we edged along, I worried we wouldn't find the handle. I half believed my imagination, so bent on finding treasure, had dreamed it up. We stumbled upon it right away, however.

Dev gave it a tug, but it still wouldn't budge. Working together, we loosened up more of the dirt filling the cracks around the hatch. Before long, we managed to jimmy the door free.

Dev and I both aimed our flashlights downward.

"A ladder," I said. "Just like you predicted."

"You first." Dev extended his arm toward the rungs just as Cocoa let out another series of woofs. "You're the official dog-sitter."

"Right." I grasped the sides of the ladder. With shaky legs, I stepped onto the top rung and took a deep breath. Opening the door had thrilled me more than finding a geocache on Mars. I'd longed for this moment ever since I'd found the padlock in Magpie. Yet, I couldn't keep images of catacombs and dungeons from seeping into my head as I descended.

After fifteen steps my feet hit solid ground. A musty smell filled my nose. Feeling more spooked than if I'd wandered, lost, through a graveyard on a windy night, I brushed aside a tangle of sticky cobwebs and stepped forward, into the shadows. I half expected to stumble into tombs and coffins, if not chains and stretching racks littered with rotting body parts and crumbling bones.

With jittery hands, I directed my flashlight upward, illuminating the area. The ladder had brought me to a small room. Aside from some boxes stacked against the opposite wall, it stood empty.

"Was this a torture chamber?" Dev joined me after a minute. "Nothing could survive long in this stale air."

His comment made my hair stand on end. I gritted my teeth, though, and methodically scanned the room with my flashlight. Finding nothing but dust in the barren chamber, I crossed over to check out the cartons by the far wall.

I drew in a sharp breath. Before me stood, not boxes, but two chests. I stooped to inspect them. Both were closed, their lids held in place by rusty latches.

Dev turned to one and tried to free its clasp. I worked on the other, smaller one. After scraping and struggling for a few minutes, Dev finally loosened the metal and lifted the lid.

Together, we peered inside. My heart stood still. Spiders could have crawled up the back of my neck, but I wouldn't have cared. Every ounce of my attention focused on the chest. Inside it, stacked neatly in rows, lay several gold-colored bars.

We stared at them for a long moment. Soon our chests pounded, as our hearts restarted. But otherwise, we only heard Cocoa barking in the distance. Jaws dropping, we finally turned to face each other.

"Is...? Is that gold?" Dev asked.

"I think so." My voice came out strained. Reaching into the chest, I gingerly lifted a bar. "It's heavy, the way gold should be."

Dev took it and turned it over. "And it's imprinted with a crown or some official seal. It must be gold! Erin, I think there's a fortune in here! I think we've finally found it!" Dev bumped my fist, let out a holler, and hopped around in a victory dance. After returning the bar to the chest, I joined in.

After a minute I paused to catch my breath. Mrs. Kelsey had left a clue leading to the crawlspace. I couldn't fathom why she'd left me something so valuable, though. I'd expected one of her husband's old golf balls or a cracked Frisbee at best.

Dev kept dancing around. His hopping and jumping reminded me of Mrs. Kelsey constantly tapping her foot to a beat. Something didn't fit, though. Mrs. Kelsey couldn't have known about this room or its treasure. Though she loved ballet and tap, she'd admitted herself that she couldn't enter the crawlspace because of her stiff hip.

I motioned for Dev to cut the dance. "This can't be meant for us," I said. "It doesn't make sense."

"That's right," said a deep voice behind us. "It was meant for me."

* * *

I dropped my flashlight and spun around. A bright beam flooded my face, all but blocking my vision. I could just make out the silhouette of a large man looking down from the hatch. Furthermore, he appeared to be holding a short, pointy object, aimed in our direction.

"That's right, it's a gun."

I grabbed Dev's arm. Together, we stumbled backward. The deep voice sounded vaguely familiar, but I couldn't dwell on it. Never in my life had my blood curdled more violently. My heart throbbed against my chest, more powerfully than if I'd encountered a mother bear on a trail, only to realize I stood between her and her cubs.

"You've done a nice job." The man lowered himself onto the ladder and started climbing down. He held on with one hand while keeping the gun directed at us with the other. "You found this room and even pried open the chest for me."

Finally, as he stepped off the ladder, the light shifted. It illuminated his long face and pointy chin.

"Steve!" My jaw dropped.

"That's right," the man answered with a smile. "It's Steve Fogarta, the friendly guy from the neighborhood."

But we'd played ball together. He'd seen potential in my pitching!

"Sorry to drop in on you so abruptly, but I could use your help."

Though still cowering against the wall, I released my grip on Dev. My eyes darted from side to side. We needed a safe way out of here.

"Those bars are pretty heavy. Since you two have proved yourselves so capable, why don't you help me carry them back to my van?" Steve tossed us some burlap sacks.

Dev's hands shook as he took one. He'd never looked so pale.

I gulped. Dev had no plan. Though less likely than finding a difficulty five, terrain five cache in under five minutes, Dev didn't have any tricks up his sleeve, for once. I would have to come up with something.

Steve gestured for us to fill the sacks. "If everyone cooperates, I'll reward you with safety. However, if you prefer to do things your own way, this scene could get rather messy." He indicated the handgun to drive home this last point.

Marcus's recorder—I had it on me! While rummaging with a sack, I reached into my pocket and switched it on. If we could get Steve to talk, we'd get it all on tape. I just needed a way to communicate my plan to Dev.

"You must be working with Rather Be Fishing," I said. At the same time, I hiccupped, hoping Dev would recognize the Resh Renner reference. "Or you're with Fife & Drum." I hiccupped again.

Dev didn't react. But Steve did. "I don't know what you're playing at, girl." He brandished the weapon. "But unless you do as I say, there'll be consequences." He motioned toward the sacks.

Dev and I started loading bars. I hiccupped once more, louder this time. Finally I caught Dev's eye and pointed to the recorder in my pocket.

Dev gave the slightest of nods. "But... but what are you doing here?" he asked.

"Keep loading," Steve commanded. "As to why I'm here, I've simply come to claim what should have been mine a long time ago."

"What do you mean it should have been yours?" I asked.

"You've got lots of questions." Steve pointed the gun at me. "This gold was promised to me years ago by Ruby Ryker, one of the Hamiltons. Anyway, what were you going to do with it? Polish the bars for the old lady? I've had plans for this fortune for years."

"But the Hamiltons haven't lived in this house for decades," Dev said.

Steve turned the gun toward Dev. "So you think you know about the Hamiltons? Just because Erin, here, got the mowing job at Two Seventy-Five, you think you now know everything? Well let me tell you a thing or two. Ruby *Hamilton* Ryker and I go way back." Steve emphasized her middle name. "And her clan lived in this house for generations."

"The Hamiltons bought this house in 1945," I said. "They must have moved out years ago."

"Stop talking so much and keep working." Steve motioned with the pistol. "Like I said, Ruby promised me this gold years ago, even asked me to help her find it. We dreamed about our future together. We'd move out to Vegas, then take it easy."

"What happened?" Dev's nostrils flared as he spoke. But this time, I didn't make fun of him for it.

"She got herself killed. That's what happened." Steve's voice had turned husky. He straightened up. "She promised this gold to me then didn't deliver."

"But you've been after it ever since?" I asked.

"You'd better believe it. If anyone deserves this fortune,

it's me. I've built up a business in this neighborhood just to keep an eye on the house. I've spent countless hours looking for some sign of the riches. Every chance I got, I entered the house and poked around. I even risked breaking in a few times."

"But you never found anything," Dev said.

"Obviously." Steve turned and spat on the ground. "When the house went on the market a few years ago, I made an offer on it. It would have been mine, but Kelsey outbid me. So I kept watching the scene and paid a delivery woman to snoop around for me."

"Uda," I whispered under my breath.

"Then today, I knew the missus was out of town and saw you both enter the house. You'd mentioned something about clues leading here, so I waited in my van across the street."

A frenzied look filled Steve's eyes as he glanced at the bulging sacks. Dev and I had finished loading everything and stood as motionless as one of Mrs. Kelsey's glittery gold figures.

"After a while, I sneaked in the front door."

"How'd you get in?" I asked.

Steve laughed. "You two left it unlocked." He shook his head in disbelief. "Cocoa barked up a storm, but apparently not enough to get your attention, so I shut her in a bedroom and headed downstairs. When I heard voices coming from the washroom, I went into the crawlspace. And now you've done the hard part for me, locating the gold." Steve pulled his fist down in victory. "Teamwork! I don't know how I'll ever thank you. In fact, I won't. I'll be out of here in no time."

"So you didn't follow any geocaching clues?" Dev asked in spite of Steve's delirious expression, which, together with his pointy chin, made him look like a rabid rodent.

"What?" Steve stared at Dev in disbelief. "What did you say?"

"Have you ever been geocaching?" Dev persisted.

"Geo-what?" Steve barked. "Don't even think about messing with me. It looks like you need another job, handsome. Help me open the other chest."

Dev bent down and started pulling and jiggling on the rusty latch. While Steve watched him, I sneaked a peek at the recorder. Then my knees nearly gave way. The light was off. Its batteries had died.

* * *

Steve and Dev opened the chest's lid. Still keeping the gun aimed in our direction, Steve rummaged through the contents, pulling out a wedding veil, a jug, a framed picture, and a painted box.

I checked the recorder again. It was definitely not working. Marcus had recorded the sounds of all our toilets for a school project comparing low and high volume flushes. He must have run it down then. We'd probably gotten nothing of what Steve had said.

Steve combed the bottom and sides of the chest for hidden panels. Finding nothing, he returned everything, closed the lid, and pushed the chest aside. "One man's treasure is another man's junk."

He turned to Dev. "You, big guy. You get to carry the sacks." He pointed toward the hatch. "You first up the ladder. I'll hand you the gold once you're near the top. Any funny business and I'll shoot your friend." When he pointed the gun at my face, Dev raced up the ladder.

Steve handed him the sacks and made me go next. As I reached the top and crouched down in the crawlspace, the recorder fell out of my pocket.

Before I could pick it up, Dev saw that it had stopped. "No!" he yelled.

Steve sprang up the last few rungs. "What's going on?" He shifted the gun back and forth between me and Dev.

Neither of us said anything.

"Why did you yell?" Steve trained the gun on Dev. He and I glanced at each other but remained silent.

Instead of growing more hostile, Steve then reacted with an eerie tranquility. Slowly, he edged closer to Dev. The rabid rodent look gone, a dead serious expression covered his face. In a deliberate movement, he extended his arm and stuffed the gun into Dev's nose.

"Feel like telling me now?"

My breathing grew shallow, and my heart pounded in my chest. I had to do something. I didn't care if Steve bound and gagged me and left me to decompose in the crypt-like dungeon room until Cocoa's barking alerted the neighbors. I just couldn't bear the thought of Dev getting shot.

"It was me!" I said. "This fell out of my pocket." I held up the recorder.

Steve lowered the gun and took the gadget. "A Resh Renner voice-recorder, invisible-ink-decoder, lock-picker?"

I bit my lip and nodded.

Steve snorted. Then he seemed to remember he was holding a gun. "Looks dead," he said, after clearing his throat. "But who knows what it picked up earlier. Think I'll hold onto this."

Dev and I didn't attempt anything else in the crawlspace. Once we reached the washroom, Steve tied me to an exposed beam with some rags. He then ordered Dev to carry the gold to his van. With the gun in his back, Dev complied.

"You're lucky," Steve said once they'd returned and he'd tied Dev up. "No one's gotten hurt." He headed toward the doorway. "Oh, and I wouldn't bother calling the cops. Even if you report every detail of what happened here, no one will believe you."

With a smile and a wink, he then stepped through the door. After a moment, we heard the front door click shut.

Working feverishly, Dev and I cut through the rags binding us by rubbing against a rough edge of the beam. Dev then rushed upstairs.

"You're not calling the police, are you?" I yelled.

"Of course I am. We finally found the gold, and that dolt stole it right out of our hands!"

"But what will you tell them?" I caught up to Dev just as he lifted the receiver.

Dev opened his mouth but stood silent for a moment as if my realization had just hit him by telepathy. "That we were taking treasure from the crawlspace but Steve stole it from us, so they should arrest him and not us?" Dev's hesitant tone admitted defeat. He put down the phone. "But why can't we just tell them the truth?" He picked it up again. "That we were hoping to find the treasure then show it to Mrs. Kelsey?"

"Is that the truth?

Dev didn't answer.

"Even if it is, they would never believe us. We could have shown it to her when she was in the house. Why did we wait until she was away?"

"Because she never would have believed us if we talked about treasure."

"And neither will they believe us," I said.

Dev gestured helplessly. "Couldn't we just say that he robbed Mrs. Kelsey while holding us at gunpoint?"

"What would we say he stole?" I shook my head. "Mrs. Kelsey has never seen the crawlspace. She can't confirm he took the gold."

Though harder to swallow than Marcus's humongous multivitamins shaped like Resh Renner, Steve had a point. There was no use in reporting the crime. No one would buy our story. Furthermore, we risked incriminating ourselves by involving the authorities. We felt as helpless as if our hands were still tied.

Chapter 16

My waterlogged sneakers squished like wet sponges the next day as I plodded through puddles to fetch a ball. The rain beat down on my back as I threw a pitch to Dev. In spite of the weather, he'd convinced me to go to the ballpark. He must have realized I had nothing to live for anymore besides softball. Everything else I'd put my hope in over the past few months had vanished.

"Let's take a break," Dev called out from home plate. "There's a new cache in the dugout. Fife & Drum put it there."

Even that news didn't cheer me up. I just trudged through the mud toward the bench. I could now forget about Dad coming home. Mom would keep working long hours with no time for Marcus and me. Dad would move from one job to another. He'd work wherever he could but not near Northlawn.

I scraped mud from my sneakers with a stick as Dev looked around for the cache. I didn't feel like helping him search. My family would never go geocaching again.

"Got it!"

I didn't watch as Dev opened the container. My family would also never adopt a dog or build another hideout.

"Erin, check this out." Dev held out the log book.

Finally I looked up from my muddy sneakers. Someone

had taped a photo inside the book's cover. I took a closer look. My eyes narrowed.

"It looks like Mrs. Dearg." It showed a red-haired, large-nosed woman holding a flute. Next to her stood a man with a bass drum strapped to his front.

"Yeah, but it says it's Fife & Drum."

"What?" I grabbed the log book. "Here we are at a competition with the Hilland Highlanders," read the caption.

I gasped. "She must be Fife!" I pointed to Mrs. Dearg. "And he must be Drum." I indicated Mr. Dearg.

"Which makes sense. She's always talking about marching band competitions."

"And she's always wearing '80s clothes. Remember? They set up that '80s-themed cache."

"Right."

"And they once posted a log about winning the big prize." I scratched my head. "I thought they were talking about the treasure."

"But they must have meant first place in a band competition."

My head dropped to my chest, and my shoulders sagged. "We were so off."

"Yup."

"And we never suspected Steve, either."

"Yup again. We even played ball with him, right here on this field."

I gazed out at the muddy diamond and shook my head. "I can't believe he took everything after we searched for so long. He thinks it belongs to him just because he knew the Hamiltons."

"And he didn't even feel bad about tossing the family heirlooms aside."

All the stuff Steve had found in the small chest came to mind. He'd taken out a veil first. Probably once white, it had looked yellow as he'd fingered its frail lace. Then he'd removed a cracked, brown jug. I remembered something else, too: a picture frame. He'd barely glanced at it. He'd just set it aside and lifted out a box—a small wooden box, one that sort of looked like Magpie, Macaw, and Quail.

"But if Fife & Drum is the Deargs, who's the babysitter?" Dev was still staring at the picture.

I grabbed his arm. "It doesn't matter. There's something more important. The missing music box is there in the crawlspace!"

Dev looked like a wild pitch had hit him in the head.

"With Steve's gun in my face yesterday, I didn't give it any thought. But now I'm sure of it. We saw the fourth box yesterday, and it's still in the crawlspace."

* * *

Dev and I lost no time in returning to Mrs. Kelsey's.

We headed downstairs. This time, we made sure to lock the front door first. After locating the loose insulation panel, I set it aside and slithered through the opening into the dusty, dark beyond.

Dev followed me into the dank and musty chamber. The chests still stood against the far wall. We opened the smaller one. On top lay the framed photograph.

"Must be the Hamiltons," Dev said.

I studied it for a second but then set it aside. Dev pulled out the veil and the jug in the meantime. Next he lifted out the box.

It looked like an antique version of Magpie, Macaw, and Quail. A bird was delicately painted on its top, the color cracked and faded. It had brown feathers and long feet, but I didn't recognize the species. Dev turned the box around. A crank poked out of its back.

My heart thumped so hard, I swore its movements were stirring up dust in the air. "It's a music box."

"What does it mean, though? If that box completes the puzzle, it must lead to the treasure. But we already found the gold."

"And lost it."

"Something doesn't make sense."

Dev opened the lid. We found nothing inside, but he turned it over. Searching in the dim, dusty beam of light, he probed and poked until a panel slid off. Just as with the other boxes, a word lock peered out at us.

Dev handed it to me. "It's all yours. Do your thing with the notes."

I wound the crank. A few notes pinged through the air. Then the box paused as it geared up to play the tune again from the beginning. Starting low, its pins plucked its melody. It didn't stop after six notes, however. It kept going. In fact, it seemed to play a complete song.

I gulped. The lock only had six dials. Still, the tune sounded hopeful, although maybe a little sad, too. More significantly, it resolved nicely at the end, unlike the other boxes' music.

It also sounded familiar, or most of it did. I turned the crank and listened again as Dev started scraping at something on the wall. The box played all three melodies the other boxes played, one after the other. It joined them together into one piece and then added a fourth, new line. The new part had six notes. Maybe they would do the trick on this box.

Ignoring the grunts, hmm's, and oh's that were escaping Dev's mouth, I hummed some scales until I figured out the new sequence: A-C-G-A-G-E.

I spun the dials while Dev brushed away at the far wall. My breath caught in my throat as I pulled on the lock.

Nothing moved.

I pulled again, harder. Still, the lock wouldn't budge. Checking the dials, I noticed the first one had slipped. I set it back to A and pulled on the lock once more.

This time, I felt a satisfying click as it opened.

As if handling a precious work of art, I lifted the lid of the compartment. Inside I discovered a key wedged into the bottom.

"I found a doorway," Dev announced. I looked up. By brushing away dirt, he had laid bare a door's frame in the far side of the room. "There's a padlock, though, and it won't budge."

My gaze shifted from the key in my hand to the door and back. "I think I have the key." I pried it loose. "It was in the box's hidden compartment."

"Try it out."

My fingers trembled as I inserted the key into an ancient-looking padlock on the door. I gave it a turn.

Something clicked.

Pulling gently, I unhooked the lock. Dev then opened the door, revealing a passageway leading into darkness.

* * *

Dev and I aimed our flashlights into the void. My skin crawled with an eerie energy. Maybe we'd found a system of catacombs. The flashlight beams didn't reach far. My next step might trigger a hidden trap or plunge me into a bottomless pit.

"It looks like a tunnel." Dev leaned in to inspect the rough, circular wall. "Or some concrete piping."

"I wonder where it leads."

"Yeah, and why it's here." Dev sniffed the air. "I hope it never held sewage."

I shone my light further. "Remember when I told you about the bomb shelter the Hamiltons built?"

"Yeah, maybe."

"I wonder if this was part of it." I took a hesitant step into the narrow, low-ceilinged area and grazed the unfinished walls. I hoped the tunnel segments wouldn't slide apart as we advanced, revealing a hall of mummies.

"Or maybe the room with the chests was the shelter." Dev scratched his chin. "Maybe this tunnel is just another way out."

Images of linen strips and amulets haunted me. I ventured further anyway. I scanned the tunnel walls with my flashlight, hoping not to spot tomb art. Caught up in visions of urns filled with bodily organs, I ended up bumping into something solid on the ground.

I sprang back, convinced I'd stumbled upon a sarcophagus. My flashlight beam only illuminated a small shelf, though. I leaned in closer. Standing to the side of the tunnel, it held several ancient-looking cans of food.

Dev picked one up. "String beans?"

I grabbed a can and studied its label. "This must have been their emergency supplies, in case they were stuck here."

"Yeah, but beans?" Dev fanned his nose. "Not what I'd stock in my unventilated shelter."

I let out a laugh as I pictured people huddled in an underground room, starting to get hungry but not wanting to open the beans. Then, thoughts of the Hamiltons brought back memories of Opal's diary. I peered beyond the shelf. The tunnel wound to the right and disappeared into darkness. It kind of looked like the dark maze in the "Lost in the Labyrinth" video game. Suddenly, though, I knew

I could navigate its twists and turns. Based on what I'd read in the diary, I felt sure of the way to proceed.

"I think this leads to the neighbors." I stepped further into the tunnel. "Remember when I told you about the tunnel network the Hamiltons had that led to the neighbors' houses?"

"No." Dev batted at a tangle of cobwebs that had attacked his shoe. "But I'm all ears now."

"All the houses on this block were built in the same style at the same time. If the Hamiltons had a bomb shelter, their neighbors might have had them, too. Maybe the tunnels connect them."

Thoughts of caskets and skeletons forgotten, I forged ahead, following the dimly lit passage for several more feet, until it ended in a T-intersection. "We've moved south of the house," I called back to Dev. "I think we're somewhere beneath the street."

"Wow. You have a great sense of direction."

"No." I waved my wrist. "My watch just has a compass." I turned left and led the way east.

After several hundred feet, a tunnel veered off to the right. "Let's see where this goes." The passageway continued for a while but then ended.

Dev and I knocked and pushed on the solid surface blocking our path. He shook his head. "It's sealed off."

We turned back and returned to the piping underneath the street. This time, we headed west. Soon we found more tunnels leading off to the right and left. Each one we explored ended abruptly in a concrete slab.

"Why would someone build tunnels that lead nowhere?" I stopped to flick a critter off my arm.

"I think you're right about the tunnels going to the neighbors." Dev looked around. "If this main tunnel runs

75 Hidden Path Drive

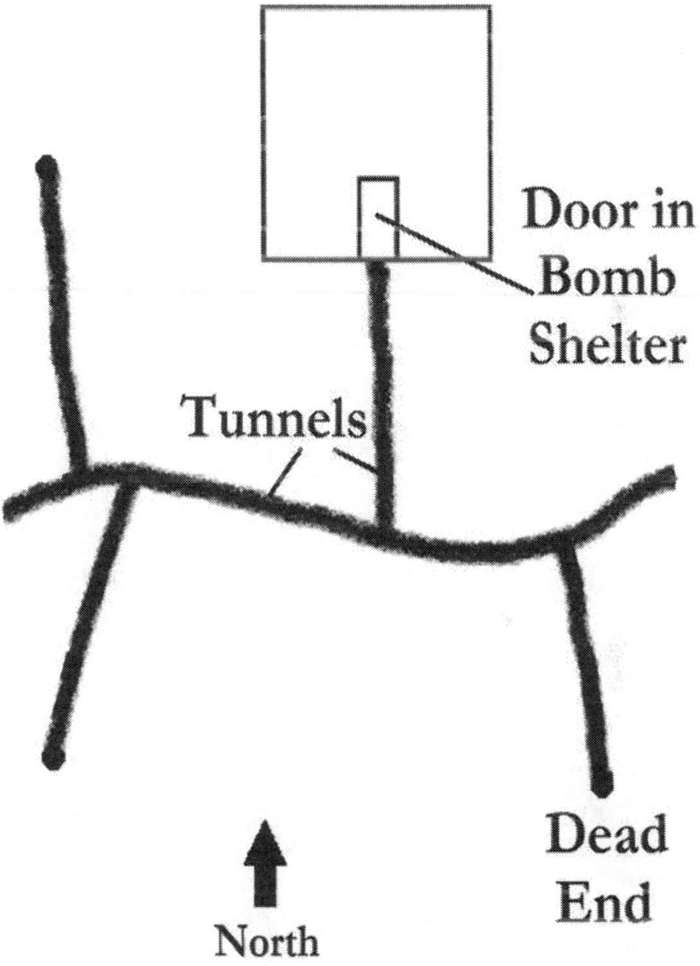

below the street, maybe the side tunnels go to each of the houses."

In my mind I tried to picture everything on a map. What Dev said made sense.

"Maybe that's why it's called Hidden Path Drive," I said.

"Yeah, and Mystery Hills Lake is right around the corner. I wonder what's under it."

I thought of dank, dripping caves and underground rivers for a second but then frowned. "Why doesn't anyone know about this now?" I pinched my arm to make sure my imagination hadn't switched into overdrive.

"Maybe the Hamiltons were the only ones who used their shelter." Dev examined the concrete that blocked our path. "They might have carved a door leading into the tunnels, but maybe the neighbors never used their shelters, then forgot about them."

"Wouldn't people know if there was a bomb shelter under their house?"

Dev flapped his lips. "Supposedly there's a crawlspace under our house, but we've never been in it. People probably just forgot about the tunnels back then if they never used them. And now no one has any idea they exist."

I reached up and grazed my hand along the tunnel roof. "Still, this is amazing."

We turned back toward Two Seventy-Five. I wondered what Dad would think of this underground wonder now that he had experience in subterranean worlds. My heart fluttered as I pictured him leading a team of hard hats through this maze.

Then I thought of Opal's diary again, with its talk of underground passageways. And an idea hit me. In fact, it nearly knocked me over, as if I'd bumped my head on the concrete. Without a doubt I now knew the way out of the maze. I'd figured out how to reach the end not just of this underground network but of the dark labyrinth that had imprisoned me since Dad had left.

"Wait a second," I called to Dev. We'd reached the chamber with the chests. "Before we head back to the house, let's check something out." I turned back into the tunnel and groped along the side of the curved concrete wall. "I think there's a hidden entrance here somewhere."

* * *

"You read about this, too, didn't you?" Dev followed close behind.

"Yeah, the diary mentioned it, or hinted at it."

Shining our lights along the dark passageway, we searched for uneven sections. The rough concrete made it hard to find anything. Every crevice looked like a gap leading to another tunnel. We pushed and scraped but got nowhere.

Soon we stumbled into the shelf with the beans again.

I stared at it. "We need to look behind that shelf," I said. Countless geocaching outings had taught me to recognize a good hiding place. I began piling up cans of beans, beets, and pearled onions on the ground. Dev helped. Next we scooted the shelf away from the wall.

Feeling along the rough concrete, I found another crevice. It felt deeper and shifted a little when I applied some pressure. Dev and I pushed and scraped away at it. Before long, we'd loosened a section of the wall. Pushing some more, we created an opening.

Dev motioned to me to enter first. I felt light-headed, as if hundreds of helium balloons had lifted me into the air. Somehow I crawled through and came out in another chamber.

Before allowing myself a glimpse of what it held, I closed my eyes and mentally retraced our steps. Discovering this room confirmed my suspicions. Following the same design they'd used on the farm and recorded in the diary, the Hamiltons had built a storage area in this house. A secret passageway had branched off to the room I now stood in.

My entire body shook as I finally opened my eyes and took in the room's contents. According to the diary, the Hamiltons had stored valuables in this area on the farm. My fading flashlight beam made it hard to see, but it looked like they'd also stashed riches here, but no mere farmer's savings. Instead, a ginormous treasure chest stood at my feet.

Dev made a sound like trumpet fanfare as he crawled through the opening. Then he gasped.

I stumbled toward the chest and lifted its lid, afraid it would disappear at my touch. When it simply opened, my knees gave way. From what I could see, the chest held mounds of jewels and stacks of gold bars.

I turned to Dev and opened my mouth, but no words came out. Practically slobbering, I returned to the chest, this time spotting a hoard of silver coins.

Dev joined in the fun. Together we sifted through rings, tiaras, scepters, and piles of jewels. Like little kids diving into presents under the tree on Christmas morning, we grabbed, gaped, and squealed.

Finally I found my voice. "The Hamiltons must have copied the design of their farmhouse storage rooms."

"What do you mean?" Dev held up a silver goblet and examined it in his flashlight beam.

"They stashed some gold bars in the bomb shelter but hid the lion's share of their fortune deep in the tunnels. Anyone entering their shelter would take the gold and run, never suspecting they'd buried more treasure behind secret passageways."

"Whatever. This is unbelievable!" Dev looked up from staring at a Wiffleball-sized ruby.

"Yeah, there's enough treasure here for a long winter break in Hawaii."

"Are you kidding? There's enough to buy an entire fleet of hover-mobiles in Resh Renner's world."

"Mrs. Kelsey will have a stroke when she hears about all this, right under her house." With a jewel-bedecked saber in my hand, I went through a few fencing moves. "Here." I held another sword out to Dev. "Join in."

He didn't take it. Instead, he stopped sifting through the chest and stared at me. I gestured with the sword again, but he didn't move. Then he tossed a silver coin up in the air and caught it. "Um, Erin, you're not going to tell Mrs. Kelsey about all of this, are you?"

"Of course I am." I straightened up out of my fencing stance. At the same time, my grip on the saber tightened. "Of course we are. Aren't we? I mean, this is her house." I looked at the wealth that lay unguarded at our feet.

"Yeah, but... I mean... I don't know. It just seems like we both need the money more than she does." Dev's hand brushed the top of the chest. "And she doesn't know about any of this."

"That doesn't matter." I twisted a curl. Or did it?

Dev shrugged. "With all these riches, your dad could buy enough plane tickets to come home every weekend." He scooped up a handful of coins and let them spill back into the trunk. "And it's not like Mrs. Kelsey would miss anything."

I stared open-mouthed at him as I fingered the jewels on the saber's hilt. Then my gaze wandered to the chest.

Right there, within reach, was everything I'd hoped for since my dad had left. Not only could these riches reunite my family, they could provide us with a better life. We could have a hideout and a yard again.

My flashlight flickered, and its beam glinted off the sharp edge of the saber. Then again, by making plans, was I inviting danger?

"Awesome." Dev's voice interrupted my thoughts. He'd pulled out some armor.

"Cool." I joined him and we tried it on. We then sifted through more coins, gems, gilded volumes, and jewelry. We even found a collection of shields and crowns, which we modeled for each other. Still, nothing could erase the tension in the air.

At some point, I looked at my watch. "Whoa. It's late. We'd better get back before anyone suspects anything."

"Yeah." Dev took off a breastplate he still had on.

We returned everything to the chest. On our way back through the tunnels, we made sure to seal up the secret entrance and lock the door leading from the bomb shelter. Once we reached the washroom, we also boarded up the crawlspace entrance and moved some storage bins in front of the loose panel. We avoided discussing the treasure, though. Finally, we split up to ride home.

Chapter 17

I couldn't sleep that night. For at least an hour I counted sheep, then quail, magpies, and macaws. Then I turned from side to side like a sunbather trying to get an even tan. After fluffing my pillow for the hundredth time, I finally got up, found Uncle El's contact on my phone, and opened a text window.

Not sure how to begin, I merely sat for a moment, twisting a strand of hair. Finally, my mind spewed out conflicting, jumbled up thoughts.

> *Erin: We finally found the treasure, loads of it. And everything was clear at first. Of course I'd tell Mrs. Kelsey. Then Dev said maybe we shouldn't.*

Maybe he was right. That room held everything I needed to get my old life back. Dad would come home. We'd have time for geocaching and practicing pitching and working on archaeology projects.

I detangled my hand from my hair. I'd twisted it so much, it probably looked like curling ribbon someone had run over a scissor edge one too many times.

> *Erin: Mrs. Kelsey would never miss*

anything. Could we just take a little? She even encouraged us to poke around with her treasure hunts.

She'd even left a clue leading to the crawlspace.

Erin: Still, there's no way she knew about the riches.

The Hamiltons knew about the fortune, but The Bird Watchers never answered mail. Steve knew the Hamiltons but didn't know about the geocaching clues.

I shook my head, banged my elbows down on the desk, and planted my face in my hands. My turmoil only increased when techno music blasting from a neighbor's stereo throbbed against my ears.

Chancing a glance at my screen after a long moment, I saw that Uncle El had already replied. He'd sent me a link to online photos.

I detached a numb finger from a tight curl and opened it. It led to a page filled with shots of Mrs. Kelsey: one of her dancing, some at an art show, another with someone who might be her daughter. One by one I browsed through the photos. Memories of Mrs. Kelsey and her pizzazz came to mind. I pictured her drum set and the Latin beats she loved, her fuchsia reel mower, her gold glitter spray cans, her tiaras, the treasure hunt clues penned in purple ink, her pottery wheel, and the clay smudged in her hair.

The slightest of smiles crept onto my lips. I didn't care how Uncle El had accessed the site. Anything's possible when your friends include Internet executives. Instead, I focused on Mrs. Kelsey. There was no forgetting her quirky style.

Erin: I can't cheat Mrs. Kelsey, can I?

Even if she didn't know about the fortune, I couldn't just help myself to whatever I wanted. Still, another question bothered me.

Erin: But what about Dad?

If we wanted him home, we needed money. And the treasure would easily solve that problem.

I stared at my phone for a while, but Uncle El didn't answer. I tossed it onto my bed. Then another thought hit me. My actions didn't just affect Mrs. Kelsey. The Hamiltons actually owned everything.

The Bird Watchers! I threw up my arms, yanking out some hair in the process.

The BirdWatchers had never answered e-mail, but they must know the Hamiltons.

Giving up on sleep, I opened a browser and pulled up the The Bird Watchers' profile on the geocaching web site.

The Bird Watchers

Profile Information: I wake with the lark song, hopefully before the swan sings.

Was that a lark on the fourth box? I could still picture the painting on its lid, with its dull-colored bird and clumps of grass. Google confirmed that larks build nests out of grass on the ground and that their feathers blend into the surrounding dirt and camouflage them.

The profile talked about larks singing. I started to research chirps and tweets, but then I realized the lark had already sung. After I'd wound it, the box had played its music in the secret room. But The Bird Watchers would never know unless someone told them. I began writing an e-mail.

> *Hi, The Bird Watchers,*
> *The lark sang this afternoon. It played these notes: C-D-F-E-D-C-G-C-D-F-E-A-B-C-D-C-G-A-A-C-G-A-G-E.*

The profile's next line read, "Hopefully before the swan sings." This time, Google reported that a swan song describes a final act or appearance, since swans are rumored to only sing just before their death.

My stomach sank, as if I'd swallowed a gold nugget. The swan song must refer to death. Perhaps The Bird Watchers hadn't answered my mails simply because they'd died.

Pushing that idea aside, I finished the mail.

> *Please reply. Please tell me the swan hasn't sung yet.*
> *Water Break*

I bit my lip and drew in a nervous breath of air as I clicked *Send*. I'd put together the clues and found the treasure, but the mystery still nagged at me. Why had the Hamiltons abandoned everything in the crawlspace? Why had they launched the music boxes?

Long after midnight, I climbed back into bed. What felt like minutes later, I woke up when the first bright rays of sun filtered through my blinds. For a second, I felt like my old self—an eighth grader who had nothing more to worry about than studying for a test on the *Atocha* shipwreck when I didn't even know which ocean it had sunk in. Then, as I stirred, the events of the previous day bulldozed back into my mind, knocking me off balance and rattling my world.

I shook off the covers, stumbled out of bed, and pleaded with my in-box to provide an answer. At last, the e-mail program came to life, announcing I had one new message. Its subject read, "Re: The lark sang." I jumped up and thumped the screen in a high-five motion. Then I held my breath and opened the mail.

* * *

My eyes scanned the message. I blinked, not trusting my vision, and scrolled down. The Bird Watchers had sent a long reply.

> *Dear Water Break,*
>
> *Congratulations. You have successfully decrypted the cache. The fact that you've contacted me also tells me you're curious about what you've found. I'll do the best I can to explain everything.*
>
> *Although you know me as The Bird Watchers, my name is Pearl Ryker. The lark box belonged to my grandmother, Opal Beryl Hamilton. Opal and my family lived at 275 Hidden Path Drive for several generations, although we trace our roots back to royalty in Scotland. That's where the story starts, with a man named Osgar Bran Harris—*

Osgar Bran Harris? Seriously? In spite of my misgivings, I kept reading. Pearl went on to explain how Osgar had robbed the Scottish royal treasury after getting on the king's bad side. Then he'd sailed to America. But instead of showing off his wealth, he'd hidden it, probably to avoid getting robbed. With land free for the taking, he hadn't spent it either. He'd just saved it in case he ever needed it in a crisis.

The tradition continued, with the fortune passing from one generation to the next although the family name changed to Hamilton at some point. They only ever dipped into their reserves when tragedy struck.

Then in 1918 the flu wiped everyone out except for Opal. She brought the fortune with her when she moved into 275 Hidden Path Drive but died before telling anyone about it.

How had Pearl found out about it, then?

> *—I didn't learn about the wealth until recently, when I came across Opal's diary and some other books chronicling Osgar's journey. I also found a photograph of Opal. On a mantel in the background sat the lark box. That image triggered a flood of memories. I could see Grandma Opal again and remembered her showing me that box, impressing upon me its importance and promising she'd share a secret with me some day. I could also hear its tune and Grandma's voice singing its song. She hummed it often, telling me if I ever faced trouble, to think of that song. I suspected it might play a significant role in unlocking her secret—*

Pearl explained that she'd wanted to search the house

but had already sold it. She'd also been hospitalized with a severe condition.

When her mother and sister Ruby passed away, she gave up hope of finding anything. Instead, she formulated a plan to get someone to hunt for her:

> *—I intended to entice a stranger into searching for the fortune, through the promise of wealth.*

My eyes grew wide. She was talking about me. I'd taken the bait and fallen into her trap.

> *When the house went on the market, I knew it was time to carry out my plan since anyone serious about finding the fortune might have a chance to access it. So I left cryptic clues in geocaches, hoping to cast a mysterious aura around the adventure and make it more alluring. I made the clues challenging and never answered e-mails since I wanted perseverance to play a key role in the hunt. Anyone who gave up too easily would never prove capable of keeping my family's custom alive.*

I shook my head. She certainly hadn't skimped on making it challenging. We'd faced everything from wasps and cryptic clues to an evening in Harold's shed.

> *You have now worked my puzzle. If the stories of Osgar are true, you have also found his fortune. I hope everything has fallen into good hands. But please don't try to find me. I only have a few months,*

> *and I have no interest in the wealth. I designed the treasure hunt simply to find an heir. Besides, I've discovered something more valuable in the meantime.*

My head lurched. Had the Hamiltons hidden more treasure somewhere?

> *Yes, I've found something truly priceless: peace. I've mastered the art of being content in any situation, whether I'm living in abundance or in need, feeling strong or weak. Through my sickness I've learned to enjoy the present moment instead of agonizing over what I've lost or letting greed consume me.*
>
> *You may not understand. Most people think money will make them happy. Perhaps illness has changed my perspective, but contentment ranks higher than affluence in my book. My family agreed. We never viewed our fortune as wealth but instead as security, resorting to it only to avert a crisis.*

I looked off to the side. Pearl's syrupy language made it hard to wrap my mind around her message, but slowly, her sentiment began to sink in. I remembered when Dev and I had finally located the Hamilton house only to learn someone lived there.

At that point, we pretty much gave up on finding treasure. But even then, I'd realized I'd already found something valuable in having Dev as a friend. We'd had so much fun tracking down clues and working on the mystery.

> *Although I can't force you to adhere to the Hamilton tradition, the fact that you've contacted me is reassuring. I trust that you'll make the right choice about what to do with the fortune.*
>
> *Sincerely,*
> *Pearl Ryker*

I scooted away from my desk, blowing air from my cheeks. Part of me felt abused. Pearl had used me, after all, to find the fortune. Yet she didn't want it for herself.

Her last line echoed through my head: "I trust that you'll make the right choice." Something else also stood out: "I hope everything has fallen into good hands."

Dad needed to come home, more than ever. But things had gotten complicated. Doing the right thing now meant something to me, too. I couldn't put a price tag on that feeling, but I couldn't ignore it either.

My eyes scanned Pearl's words again: "I've found something truly priceless: peace."

I closed my eyes and rubbed my temples. Being at peace with the situation ranked pretty high on my scale, too. Who didn't want to be one with their universe?

But it came at a high cost. If I reported the treasure, I wouldn't see Dad again for a while. I also might lose Dev. He and I had never disagreed on anything before. If I told Mrs. Kelsey what we'd found, he might not hang out with me anymore. Then a chemistry would certainly bubble between him and some pretty, straight-haired girl with a sparkly phone.

Chapter 18

After navigating my way to the bathroom through a maze of Marcus's failed attempts at creating stink bombs, I took a shower. And the way forward became clear.

Dialing Dev's number, I sat on the edge of my chair.

"Hey, Erin."

"Hey, Dev." I fanned my nose, grimacing at the lingering scent of Marcus's concoctions. "I... uh." I needed to tell Dev we had to report the treasure, but the words wouldn't come out.

"You still want to give up all those riches by telling Mrs. Kelsey what we found?"

I gulped, feeling worse than if I'd gotten hit by a stink missile. "Um, well, actually..."

"Don't worry. I'm on board now, too."

My lips made weird motions as I tried to figure out what to say. "What do you mean?" I finally sputtered.

"Well... people are going to find out about the treasure. There's no way we can hide it. They'll ask where it came from. Basically they'll pester me more than they usually do until they know all the details."

I blinked a few times, trying to digest Dev's words. "Good point."

"Plus, you're right. It doesn't belong to us. And I don't know if I could live with myself if I took it."

"Yeah, me too." I swallowed hard. "So... what do we do?"

"Well, I sort of already told my cousin. She's doing some project for the historical society through a college class she's taking, and she was desperate for an idea."

"Oh."

"Anyway, she wants to come back with us and bring her professor. And the police."

The word *police* made me sit up straight but I agreed we should get some help. "Okay. I'll bring my mom, too."

"So, can we head over there right away? Or what did you call about?"

"Uh... nothing." I smiled. "Sounds great."

Dev's cousin and her professor met us at Hidden Path Drive. The cousin's boyfriend, a police officer, also showed up. Together, we toured the tunnels and treasure room.

The professor and the cop took the best part of an eternity photographing everything. They also made a big fuss about us not touching anything. It would have gotten annoying, except that they both kept commenting on how Dev and I would get credit for this remarkable discovery.

Something the professor said on the way out also helped. He didn't think the treasure had much value anymore but said, "You two will certainly get a reward for discovering the tunnel network."

I raised my eyebrows at Dev. *Credit* and *a reward* sounded good. He seemed to agree. He lifted me in a tight hug and spun me around. What exactly did those words mean, though?

We didn't find out right away, but when Mrs. Kelsey returned on Monday, the entire group assembled again. We told her the whole story.

"Stop kidding me." Mrs. Kelsey smiled as she scrutinized me. "Where's the camera? This is just one of those improv shows, isn't it? Where people tell someone something spectacular just to see their reaction?"

"No, ma'am," the professor said. "We are quite serious." He pulled out a screen and gave her a virtual tour, showing her video footage of the tunnels.

Mrs. Kelsey eyed him skeptically. Then she made the officer put his hand on a piece of pottery covered in gold sparkles and swear that we'd told the truth. Still, not until the lawyer produced some paperwork showing plans and sketches did she begin to believe us. Or we think she did because she performed a few leaps and pirouettes. Then she danced a polka with the officer.

I felt like dancing, too. We'd told everyone the truth, without taking even a tiny copper coin for ourselves. Just getting the weight of that secret off my shoulders felt like a million bucks.

* * *

Several weeks later, Mrs. Kelsey started packing. She'd made an offer on the condo in Florida. Also, the professor had convinced the university to buy her house so he could conduct research on the tunnel network.

A few days before her moving truck came, she asked me to help her finish boxing everything up. She greeted me with another treasure hunt. "I didn't make it up for you, though," she explained as she let me in. "I just need your help finding something I hid for myself years ago."

Now an expert at deciphering her clues, I worked through the hints in no time. They led to a bathroom closet. But inside, we only found a tower of pink toilet paper rolls.

On my way back downstairs I picked up a roll that had fallen to the side. Crumpled up inside the tube was a piece of paper. I pulled it out and smoothed it flat only to discover I held a one thousand Swiss franc bill.

Mrs. Kelsey took the note and held it at arm's length to study it. Then, wobbling, she reached for the sink to steady herself.

I looked in more rolls and found yet more bills, all thousand franc notes. After about the fifth one, Mrs. Kelsey slumped down onto the floor and leaned back against her neon pink toilet.

"I thought I remembered putting something away for my granddaughter's wedding." She wiped her moist eyes. "But I'd forgotten where I'd hidden it."

When her crying didn't look like it would stop anytime soon, I pulled out more Swiss bills. The bigger the stack grew, the harder she wept, but I couldn't stop laughing.

When I'd finally cleared the cabinet, I headed downstairs to pack up piles of Mrs. Kelsey's tutus, leotards, and tiaras. She kept up a steady stream of whimpers and gasps while I worked. I wondered if she'd discovered a stash of Euros, too, inside tissue boxes.

Eventually she made it down to the door. She hugged me good-bye, and I smiled all the way home. My joy only grew when I got to my room and emptied my pockets. Mrs. Kelsey had tucked a thousand franc bill into my pay.

As if my aura wasn't already glowing, more good news soon came my way. And it all happened so quickly, I felt like a whirlwind had ripped through my life. First, Dev and I got our picture in the paper when we received an eye-popping award for finding the tunnel network.

Even better, the university unveiled plans to open a park showcasing the underground maze and offered Dev and me jobs as tour guides. To celebrate, we planted a cache in one of Mrs. Kelsey's maples.

One thing topped everything else, though. Dad returned from Hawaii a few weeks later, and the university hired him as their chief archaeologist for the tunnel project.

In other words, he wouldn't soon leave for Kyrgyzstan or some other remote corner of the world. He'd found a job in New Jersey and would live at home again. We'd get to play ball together, search for arrowheads, go geocaching, and maybe even get a dog. Everything we hadn't done in the past year we'd now do—ten times a day if we felt like it.

I texted often with Uncle El, keeping him updated on everything. He always e-mailed smiling, winking faces in response, not that I needed any uplifting. The only disappointment I suffered that entire winter was not making the school softball team. And I didn't really mind because Dad and I had already gotten back to work on my fastball, making me optimistic about next season.

Sometime later, a package came in the mail. Inside was a wooden puzzle and a letter, signed "Pearl Ryker." Even though Pearl had told me not to contact her, I'd e-mailed her anyway to let her know where Osgar's fortune had ended up.

In the note, she'd enclosed a sheet of music. She wrote:

Although the lark box plays this tune, the song actually speaks of a dove—the one that returned to the ark carrying an olive branch, the one that came to symbolize peace.

The Peace Song

Grandma Opal must have kept the key to the treasure in the lark box since it led to financial solid ground, which gave us a sense of peace.

I twisted a few of the puzzle's movable pieces but couldn't work it. Several days later, though, a few sections lined up to spell Opal's initials, *O. B. H.*

As I turned the puzzle in my hand, my thumb then shifted, pressing into an upper piece. With a click, the puzzle's top popped open.

Inside its hollow middle someone had tucked a piece of red silk. When I pulled it out and unfolded it, a dozen glittering, angular gems sparkled up at me.

For a second or two, I felt dizzy. Blinking hard, I steadied myself as I held one of the dazzling stones up to a lamp. Its brilliant, multifaceted surface reflected the light. I shook my head, still not trusting my senses. Finally, I stuffed the jewels back into the silk and raced downstairs.

"They're diamonds, all right." Dad looked up from inspecting the stunning stones under a microscope. "Enough to build an empire."

The light-headed feeling returned. If Pearl had sent them to me, either she'd known how to work the puzzle, or she'd had no idea what she'd given me.

I sprinted back upstairs and sent The Bird Watchers an e-mail. Then I checked for new messages every hour.

A week later, I still hadn't heard back. I dug through the recycling bin until I found the box she'd sent everything in, but it didn't list a return address.

I went to Geocaching.com and sent another mail through the site. Then I happened to see her profile.

She'd changed the description. It now read, "The swan sings."

"No." I pushed back in my chair. My head shook as I read and reread the words. My mind understood what they meant, but my heart refused to believe them.

I'd never dealt with death before. I stared blankly ahead, not knowing what to feel or how to respond. After a while the screen saver kicked in, but it barely fazed me. Neither did the fact that I'd just inherited a fortune of my own. I simply kept staring at the monitor. I hadn't known Pearl. Still, the permanence of her swan song overwhelmed me, sending a cold shudder up my spine.

Every day over the next week I searched the newspaper for an obituary on Pearl Ryker. Nothing appeared. I would never know if she had understood what she'd done. I could only hope that by sending the diamonds, she'd told me she somehow trusted me as her heir.

* * *

I did get some other answers a few days later. While scanning the newspaper for Pearl's name, a headline jumped out at me: "Gambling Ring Busted, Northlawn Resident Arrested."

I leaned closer and skimmed through the story. It reported on a car chase. Police had pursued a white van towing landscaping equipment. They'd raced after the vehicle and its swerving load for several minutes before arresting Steve Fogarta, the alleged orchestrator of an illegal sports betting operation.

Pearl's doubts about whether money made people happy came to mind. Although Steve had gotten away with a share of the gold, he apparently hadn't found happiness. He'd only wanted more, gambling away everything he'd gained in the process. Now his greed had landed him behind bars. In contrast, Pearl had described finding peace even though she'd faced death.

On my way home from school one afternoon, I stumbled upon another answer. While stopping by the library, I spotted Rather Be Fishing talking to Dragona.

"I've been on the waiting list for several months but have heard nothing!" he insisted.

Harold still couldn't locate the diary? But I'd returned it weeks ago. I tiptoed closer. My face hidden in an open book, I peeked over a row of shelves. From there I caught a glimpse of the librarian's screen and the book cover it displayed: *Guarded Recipes–The Trout Sushi Craze*.

Realization struck me like a splash of cold lake water after a warm, sleepy afternoon of fishing. Harold had never tried to check out Opal's diary. Instead, he'd merely wanted a book on trout sushi. At the farmer's market, he must have promised a vendor that he'd deliver sushi. And at the lake, he'd been fishing for trout and skinning his catch before delivering it to the market. Instead of plotting our murders, he'd simply been angry with Dev and me for diminishing his haul by making such a ruckus throwing rocks.

Something still bothered me, though, like a fly buzzing around a picnic table on an otherwise perfect summer day. We'd never figured out the baby-sitter's geocaching name. But we'd definitely seen her following clues, receiver in hand, on several occasions.

That evening, I found a web site listing local geocachers. Among others, I clicked on Chain Cacher, thinking the name sounded familiar. When a photo of a woman with unending hair and a toddler appeared on my screen, my eyes nearly popped out.

I checked her statistics and had to steady myself on my desk. She'd logged 5,233 finds.

She must have cached all the time, even on the job. Apparently as addicted to the sport as a chain-smoker is to cigarettes, she sneaked in a few finds whenever she took the kid out. At least she'd included his picture in her profile. I laughed at myself for ever thinking the toy tank could pose a threat.

At that point, my face ached from the grins that perpetually covered it. My pain only increased, though. A few months later, the ownership of my family's apartment changed hands, and the buyer lifted the ban on pets.

We immediately adopted Mocha, a shelter dog who reminded me of Cocoa. True to the reputation of man's best friend, she quickly became my constant companion. She followed me to the ballpark and on geocaching hikes. She even accompanied me to work at the Hidden Path Drive Tunnel Park, where I'd started prepping for my summer job, giving tours.

Another welcome surprise came a few weeks later, on a day that found me in a fantastic mood. Not even the arrival of the school's summer reading list in the mail could dampen my spirits. A crowd of tourists had just entered the now open tunnel park. I couldn't wait to lead my first tour and reveal the secrets the house had hidden for so many years.

Just after I got started, my stomach lurched. Pierce had joined the group at the last minute. Even so, I didn't let myself get flustered. Delving into the history of the house and its passageways, I smiled broadly and continued with the talk, not missing a single detail.

Afterward, he approached me. "I guess you've moved beyond romances to action and adventure."

I frowned at him, not sure of his intentions.

"You make it sound like you dug the tunnels yourself," he explained.

"Uh... thanks."

"Hey, that looks like Mr. Schmidt, the guy who runs Slivers & Shards, the archaeology camp." Pierce pointed across the room toward my dad, who had just stepped into the house. "I love that camp."

"Yeah, me too." I eyed Pierce suspiciously, wary of his next move. But if he liked archaeology, he must have some potential. I decided to try a new strategy. "Have you ever found the cache in the yard?"

"The cash? Like money?" Pierce narrowed his eyes. "What do you mean?"

"No, the cache, as in geocaching."

When Pierce just stared blankly, I pointed toward the door. "Come on. I'll show you."

Dev, who had just come back with his tour, joined us, just as I started explaining the basics of geocaching. Together, the three of us then headed out, two young fanatics eager to win another convert to their favorite sport.

Chapter 19

I found my door shut that night as I climbed the stairs to my room. When I opened it, a blast of bubbles hit me in the face. I ducked and tried to swat them away, but a whirling contraption blew a constant stream in my direction. I stepped back, only to find myself already oozing with sticky goo. Worse, bubbles covered everything: arrowheads on my desk, rubrics and agendas from last year, the piles of laundry on the floor. The entire room glistened with airy, slimy blobs.

Dev and Marcus then appeared in the hallway, grinning like monkeys. Dev had recruited my brother to finally get his revenge.

After shooing them both out the door, I flopped down on my bed and opened a text window on my phone. While a thunderstorm flashed and crashed outside my window, I thought back to the beginning of eighth grade, when I'd felt as volatile as a turbulent sky, with Dad away. Now, leaning back on my pillow, I could still feel my face glowing with the warmth, excitement, and fun of the afternoon. The scene had shifted dramatically. Not only had I discovered a fortune, I'd also turned it in. Somehow, though, I'd still benefited from it in a gargantuan way.

Erin: Thanks, Uncle El

A deluge of images rushed through my mind: the treasure room with its sparkling riches; Mocha, now resting at the foot of my bed; my dad, now home, asking me to help him prep the camp opening; and Pierce, who I'd taken geocaching.

Erin: Thanks for everything.

A low, guttural sound rumbled.

Maybe Mocha had growled with hunger. But she didn't look like she needed a bone.

It sounded again—a throaty utterance, as if a giant were chuckling.

Looking up, I finally found the source of the noise: Uncle El had initiated a video session. Visible on my screen, Uncle El sat in an astronomically large multimedia studio, positioned behind its infinitely complex controls. Tall shelves surrounded him, stacked high with DVDs, video tapes, reels of film, and audio cassettes, plus an entire library of books. Beyond those, I spotted countless database servers and external hard drives, humming away. File cabinets overflowing with documents filled the background. To the side, large screen monitors flashing and beeping with applications covered an endless wall. Speakers, microphones, and cameras galore lined a desk. An open closet door revealed heaps of microfiches and x-rays. I even thought I caught sight of some scrolls and stone tablets piled in a corner.

When Uncle El chuckled again, I turned back to face him. A huge grin spread across his face along with a smug expression that seemed to say, "Oh, I'm not done yet. Just wait and see what else I've got in store for you."

Later that evening, I thought back to Pearl's e-mail, when

she'd talked about having found peace, a treasure she considered more valuable than riches.

The thought of selling the diamonds and then spending thousands on Resh Renner gadgets, just to get Dev to stop nagging me, had certainly tempted me over the past few months. I'd also toyed with the idea of moving out of our cramped apartment and back into a house. Yet in spite of the potential glitz and comfort, I'd checked the diamonds into a vault, having decided to carry on the Hamilton tradition of saving the wealth.

The newspaper article on Steve showing the effects of greed kept coming to mind, convincing me of the dangers of rolling in cash. Plus, I couldn't really complain about things anymore. With Dad working close to home and my own summer job providing a steady flow of funds, my needs were met. Dad had also lined up another job here in New Jersey, to start in the fall. Basically, monetary concerns had fled my mind as quickly as thoughts of Mrs. Dearg's mind-rattling history exams had vanished after the last day of school.

One afternoon a few weeks later, Mocha and I climbed up to the park office after wrapping up the day's last tour. Earlier, we'd convinced the university to construct a tree house in one of Mrs. Kelsey's maples to house our tour guide office.

We found Dev already lounging in a chair, paging through the latest catalog of Resh gear and sipping baobab juice. Apparently he didn't get enough of that stuff at the cafeteria during the school year. Shaking my head, I gave Mocha a pat and peered out the window through the branches of the majestic maple.

At the moment, I couldn't imagine much more than giving tours, hanging out in the tree house, and geocaching with Dev.

Nearly as hooked as Chain Cacher, Dev had informed me we were finding a geocache every day that summer. I also found it fun on warm summer evenings to sit in the tree house, concocting a system of clues, like Pearl had, leading to treasure.

Gazing out the window, I dreamed of encoding the address of the vault holding the diamonds. I'd secure it with an ancient padlock and hide it at the final site of a multi cache, with a different puzzle to solve at each stage.

Maybe I'd launch its key as a trackable with the goal of traveling from one mystery cache to another. My mind brimming with endless possibilities, I didn't even object when Dev offered me some black rice chips with kale dip. Instead I smiled.

Like Pearl, I'd found peace.

The End

About Jennifer Kirsch

An avid geocacher, Jennifer Kirsch has reached into sewers, tugged on wads of chewed bubblegum, and dodged cactus spines while searching for geocaches. While not wading through smelly swamps or wandering into caves in the pursuit of yet another hidden container, she freelances as an editor and writer and has published several articles, including pieces in magazines with national circulation.

In past lives she has worked as a software developer, a substitute pianist, an algebra tutor, and a bagel shop clerk. Her current hobbies include making lists, reading *Dummies* books, and holding cooking contests with her husband and two daughters.

Visit her online at: www.jenniferkirsch.net.

Made in the USA
Middletown, DE
01 September 2024

60199189R00128